D1707601

Knitting in Jamaica
Author: Gary Thomas Edwards
Cover Design: Gary Thomas Edwards
Editor: Jennifer Garvey & Chelsey Clammer
Golden Shovel Publishing
© Copyright 2022, Gary Thomas Edwards, all rights reserved.
First Printing: January 21, 2023
Printed in the USA, KDPAmazon.com
Contact: knittinginjamaica@gmail.com
Social Media: www.facebook.com/bookofbob

A May Ling Chan Murder Mystery

Knitting in Jamaica

Gary Thomas Edwards

For Don

Stab it,

strangle it,

rip out its guts,

throw it off a cliff.

When Bad Days Go Bad

From somewhere deep in the bliss of being half asleep, May Ling managed to answer her phone. She didn't want to. It was so warm and comfortable spooning with Soomee. She knew all too well that a call this late at night or early in the morning (she wasn't sure what time it was) meant only one thing, some unfortunate soul had a less-than-desirable encounter with the reaper. They didn't call her at this hour to have her investigate a convenience store robbery. No, May Ling knew as she held the phone to her ear, preparing to speak, someone had died this evening at the hands of another.

"Inspector Chan," she answered, trying her best to stifle the euphoria of lying beside Soomee in hopes of sounding professional. "Yeah. Yeah. Where? Okay, give me a minute. Did you contact Soomee?" She asked, looking over at the beautiful woman sitting up and rubbing her eyes. She looked at her lovingly. "Don't bother. I'll call her and pick up her and the van on my way in."

Soomee, a rising assistant Medical Examiner at One Newhall Street in San Francisco, worked closely with Inspector May Ling Chan. They both knew their relationship was more than frowned on, that it could prove to be a conflict of interest. Or worse, it could allow some hot-shot attorney to overturn one of their cases. It could cost them both their careers.

"We have a homicide. An elderly lady. Mancini said it's a brutal one."

Soomee swung her milk-white trim legs off the bed so she could lean down and pick up her clothes. "You know you're the greatest thing that has happened in my life." she cooed. "I love you, May Ling."

"I love you too, Baby. I love my job, but it sure pisses me off when it interrupts evenings with you. Come on. I'll drop you off at the station, so you can get the van."

~~~~~~~~~~

"Who the hell would do this to a nice old lady like this, May Ling? Shit, just when I think I have seen the worst thing one human can do to another, boom, right between the eyes." Inspector Mancini said, bouncing his hand off his forehead, remarking to the lead Homicide Inspector, May Ling. She wasn't really listening while doing her best to search the half-naked woman's clothing for clues without getting blood all over her. She wasn't succeeding.

"They were definitely torturing her. They wanted something, and this tough old lady was willing to die rather than give it up." May Ling said as she ran her gloved hand through her short black hair before remembering her glove was covered in blood. "Shit!" She shouted, looking at her hand to see if blood might have transferred or if any of her hair was on the glove. "Mancini, you got another glove I can use. I just compromised this one." she sighed.

Mancini pulled his extra pair of gloves from his pocket, then, handing them to her, said, "Not to take anything away from her. I mean, this is one tough old broad for sure. But maybe she didn't have what they wanted or didn't know what they wanted. Just sayin'."

As May Ling pulled the soiled blue Nitrile glove off her hand, the glimmer from a metallic object under the small desk caught her attention. Dropping to her knees, being careful not to kneel in the pooled blood, she reached under and retrieved a small knife. She recognized it instantly as a Japanese higonokami knife. The knife, covered in blood, was still half open. On the handle, she could make out the engraved symbols enough to read Hiroto, which she knew meant *the large one*. She removed a bag from her coat pocket and dropped the knife in. "This has all the makings of a hit. These were gangbangers or gangsters. But what did they think this grandmotherly woman could have had or knew that they would torture her like this." May Ling turned her attention to the woman's head and the bloody ball of yarn stuffed in her mouth.

"Crap. Why? Soomee, I'll let you take the ball of yarn out of her mouth when you get her back to forensics. I want to know if they hid anything in the yarn or her mouth. This isn't some sicko or a serial killer. It is too messy. These were thugs, two of them, I think, judging by the footprints. But, we need to look at every angle." *Could it be as simple as a fledgling serial killer's first victim?* She grimaced as the thought passed through her mind. *Nah. No way.*

"Shit, our perp was stabbing the bottom of her feet with some kind of needle, like a knitting needle. And why cut the little toe off her right foot? I haven't been able to find it anywhere. Anyone see a toe? You know, that tells me we have a serial killer wanting to keep a memento for their first kill." the young inspector surmised.

"Thank you for noting it was they, not he or her. You're a quick study, Mancini. We don't know yet. And no, there was more than one of them. Our perps were sloppy, way too sloppy. It's too chaotic for a gang hit. I'm now leanin' toward a wannabe gangbanger kid's initiation. Anyway—" her hand froze as she started to lift the old lady's blood-soaked pink sweater.

"Oh, fuck!" was all May Ling could blurt out, looking at the dead woman's chest. Seeing far more than even her seasoned eyes could handle, she lowered the woman's sweater. *Stay calm, be cool. We'll get them by staying cool.* May Ling told herself as she forcibly controlled her breathing. She stood up and looked around the room at the variations of blood splatter on the walls, bed, and ceiling. *There's a well-written story here, thanks to them being so careless. We need to stay cool. Really cool and focused so that we can read it.* "And we will, you assholes," she said loudly toward the ceiling. "Get me more photos." She snapped to the young man with the camera. "Sorry, Jimmy, you're doing a great job kid; you always do. This one's got my attention. My full attention." She said as she looked over toward Soomee in her white Tyvek suit, kneeling next to the woman's body, "This poor soul is all yours. Get me something—" she stopped, almost saying, *baby.* "Please, get me something. I want this scum." May Ling said sternly and walked out of the house toward her car with Inspector Mancini in tow.

Soomee nodded, then turned her attention back to the deceased woman, gently touching her gloved fingers to the woman's cheek, wondering what her life had been like. Did the woman have a husband, kids, and grandkids? What did this lady do when younger, and what fate led to this horrible destiny? *No one deserves this, certainly not this woman.* She thought and shivered.

~~~~~~~~~~

9

"I'm her grandson. A detective from your department called and asked if I would come down and walk through the house to see if I thought anything was missing." Sean's head drooped as he spoke in a dispirited voice to the officer.

"Can I see some ID?" the officer asked. He looked over Sean's driver's license, squinting as he compared the photo to the young man in front of him. Then changing the look on his face, he handed back the ID. "Sorry, kid. There was simply no reason for this. We're going to find the scum who did it. They'll be held accountable." The words felt hollow coming out of his mouth as sergeant Mckenzie tried his best to comfort the young man. Years on the beat, he believed a random murder like this was likely the work of a homeless man—maybe two or three. *God knows there are enough of 'em,* he thought to himself. *Most likely a random murder for drug money and the food in the refrigerator perpetrated by a destitute person with nothing to lose, a person without a name, living off the grid in a sea of homeless humanity.* "Hang on, kid; the inspector would like to have a word with you. Stay here. I'll get her," he said and walked under the yellow tape to where several squad cars were parked.

May Ling had been an inspector working homicide for seven years. Not tall by any stretch of the imagination, her imposing stature was all attitude. Her bob cut, fitted jeans with cuffs, cotton work shirt with the sleeves rolled up but neatly pressed, and her squared-off stance made it clear she was the woman in charge. She looked up and over at Sean as she talked to the sergeant. She approached Sean confidently. "Sorry, kid," she offered first. "I'm Inspector Chan. What's your name?" she asked, nodding her head upwards with a questioning look. At the same time, she sized up the curly red-haired youth. Unlike the sergeant, she knew this was not the work of a vagrant. Nine times out of ten, it's someone the lady knew that was responsible. The highest probability is family. Standing in front of her would be the prime suspect. An older teenager or young adult who was maybe looking for drug money. Cases she had handled too many times in her career, just as this one that backed up that statistic. Except she had reviewed the crime scene and knew this was the work of more than one very sinister individual. But she had to look at every possibility. Even this red-headed kid. May Ling knew from experience that you can't take anything for granted.

"Ma'am, my name is Sean. Mary Ellen was my Seanmhair," he said, sniffling a bit and wiping his eyes that wanted to tear up but wouldn't. "I visit her a lot. I mean, I did visit her a lot." Now tears started to well up and then flow down his cheeks. "Why would anyone do this?" he pleaded more than asked.

Just like that, May Ling scratched him off her mental list of suspects. *That was just too real,* she thought. "How old are you? Do you come here often enough that you can tell if anything is missing?"

"I just turned twenty-eight. And well, yeah, I think I can. My girlfriend—can she come in and help me? She's been here as many times as me in the last year, maybe more. She and my Seanmhair were tight. They're both—" he paused as the present tense hit him. "They were both knitters and could sit and talk about knitting stuff all night. She would be more likely to see something out of place before me."

"I'm sorry, Seanmhair? What's that?" May Ling quizzed.

"Sorry, ma'am, that's how Scots say, grandmother. She would have yanked out the wooden spoon and smacked me across the top of my knuckles if I ever called her Grandma

Mary." Sean drifted off a bit, looking toward the house, his head filling with fond memories as he wiped his eyes with his sleeves.

"Sean, let me check with forensics and make sure they have everything cataloged before I let you in. Yeah, if your lady friend can help, she can go in. Don't touch anything. Just look around. Hold on, I'll be right back." *This kid looks like he could barely be eighteen with that curly auburn mop top,* she thought. She walked over to talk to a woman dressed in what looked like a white hazmat suit. The woman nodded, and May Ling headed back. "Go get your girlfriend. I want to meet her first. Gotta dot the I's, kid."

"She's right there, on the other side of the yellow tape. Kay, come here. It's okay, come here," Sean yelled, waving at her to join them.

Kaylee Wu ducked under the tape and walked toward them. Her eyes locked on Sean's. She was as distraught as he was. It was an understatement that her and Sean's Seanmhair were tight. She often came to visit without Sean just to talk about knitting. She loved Sean and knew knitting was not at all important to him. His love was computers. And his eyes lit up when you talked about any kind of history, especially ancient battles. But, she also recognized that he allowed himself to be dragged into endless shops filled with knitting supplies to fulfill her love for knitting—because he cared. It's why she loved him. Why he loved her, she wondered—a short, skinny Chinese girl with her hair dyed brilliant cyan blue wearing baggy clothes usually with holes in them—was a mystery to her. "I feel like I'm going to throw up, baby. This can't be happening. I want our Seanmhair back," she said with an emotional sigh.

May Ling stepped up, pulling a small pack of tissues

from her jacket. She offered her best comforting smile, handing Kay one, "Hi, Kay. I thought you would be Scottish or Irish hanging out with the likes of Sean here. You were born here in San Francisco, weren't you? Parents—are they from here or China?" She paused, "I am so sorry for your loss. Both of you. The only promise I will make to you is that I won't stop until I find who did this, no matter how long it takes, and I'm going to live a long time."

"Thank you, inspector. You're correct, I was born here, and my parents moved here from Hong Kong during the Korean War. My dad and mom own several small shops down on Washington, near Grant. Do you have any idea who could've done this?" Kay asked, looking her in the eyes questioningly, being they were the same challenged height.

"At the moment, no. We start by looking at family and friends first until clues lead us elsewhere. So, I hate to be the mean one here, but I need, that is if you want to help me find who did this to your grandmother; sorry, Seanmhair, I need you both to come down to the station for statements, fingerprints and swabbing. Actually, to be clear, it's not a request. Oh, and I need you to stay close, so I can find you when I need to talk to you. Got it? Questions?"

Sean and Kay nodded.

"Good. Proceed; please go inside. This officer will accompany you. Again, don't touch anything. It's still an active crime scene." May Ling turned, signaling for the officer to come over to where they were. "Sean, Kay, this is Officer Olmsted. He'll take you through the house. If you see anything important, come get me." She tried to give an encouraging smile, but it was tough to do anymore. Murder was callous business, and it had worn off her pleasant polish.

"Here, you'll need to put these on," the officer told them,

handing them each disposable gloves and booties. "I must warn you in advance your grandmother's office has not been cleaned up yet."

"Her knitting room. It wasn't an office; it was where she spent hours listening to music and knitting. I cannot imagine there would be anything in that room thieves might want. But if something is missing, I'll know it," Kay said staunchly. "Hon, if you don't want to go in that room, just wait outside the door. I understand."

"Thanks, Babe." Sean hugged her. Turning to Officer Olmsted, he asked, "When she checks out the knitting room, can I peek in the attic to see if anyone went up there?"

The officer thought about it. "Yeah, darn kid, that's a good idea. We didn't look up there. Just look, don't touch anything. If you see something, holler for me."

The three of them walked into the living room in the old Victorian. The sun at the front window filtered through the lace curtains, helping to brighten the room with its ornate vaulted ceiling. They looked around carefully, and Kay and Sean agreed nothing appeared out of place. The same held true for the kitchen, dining area, bathroom, and bedrooms. When they reached the knitting room, Officer Olmsted opened the door. "It's not pretty in there," he said to prepare Kay.

"I'm good. I want to help you find the asshole who did this," Kay said with angry conviction, preparing herself to walk in.

"Kid, as soon as you've looked up there, come straight back here." Officer Olmsted told Sean, pointing to the floor where they were standing.

"Sean. My name is Sean, sir. I will. I'll be right back. Are you sure you're okay with this, Kay?"

"Yeah, Hon. It's gotta be done. Go. Check out the attic.

I'll be fine." Kay told him as she hugged him and then turned, pausing before entering the knitting room.

As Sean headed to the end of the hall where the attic door and pull-down staircase were, he heard a loud but muffled gasp from Kay. *This piece of shit is going to pay,* he thought to himself, imagining holding a knife to the throat of whoever did this. Sean shook his head to clear his thoughts. Then he pulled the cord that released the staircase, pulling it down. He climbed to the top and pushed the small door open. Inside, Sean was able to walk on sheets of plywood laid between aging trusses. In the center, a few feet away, was a pull string for a single light bulb, which still, after so many years, did a fine job of lighting the attic. He glanced around but saw nothing that looked like it might have been disturbed. The heavy coat of dust on everything showed no signs of footprints or handprints. Sean took a deep breath, preparing to head back down, when he saw a cardboard box that would typically have held oranges. His name was written on the top and the side. He smiled, remembering it contained many toys he used to play with at the house as a kid. Without thinking, he walked over and opened it. *Shit, I wasn't supposed to do that.* He thought. *Oh well, too late now,* he defiantly thought to himself. On top of the box were several old sweaters his Seanmhair had knitted for him as a kid and one she gave him that was far too big back then. She had explained to him that it was old. She hadn't knit it; someone long ago in the family had and passed it down for future generations. *It's yours now, Sean. It's your family's heritage. She had told him to take care of it and pass it on to his eldest. Like I'm ever going to have kids*, he thought. From below, he could hear Kay calling for him. He grabbed the sweater and closed the box.

Sean climbed down, folded the stairs back up, and

returned to the hallway where Kay was sobbing. "Sean, whoever did this is a brutal bastard. Oh my God. I need to get out of here."

Officer Olmsted, seeing her distress, ushered them both outside, not noticing Sean holding a folded sweater in his arm. Inspector Chan met them as they came out. Recognizing Kay's anguish, the inspector put her arms around her, enveloping her in a long, rocking hug.

"Sorry. There is just no way to prepare someone to see something like that. But it's important. Every little detail we learn helps. You never know what simple thing out of place might be the clue that breaks the case wide open. So, thank you," she said and hugged her again. "Did either of you see anything to raise red flags?" Both shook their heads.

Sean debated if he should or shouldn't mention the box he'd opened, as he was now holding a sweater he hadn't been when he went in. Smartly and quickly, he decided the most prudent thing to do was to be totally upfront. "Ma'am, excuse me. I checked out the attic, and no one had been there before me. And—" He said, looking down and shuffling his right foot back and forth. "—I sort of opened one of the boxes. It had my name on it. It was automatic. It was the one my Seanmhair kept all my stuff from childhood. I put everything back, except—" he held out the sweater, "—this. She gave it to me. It's a very old family heirloom I'm supposed to pass down to my kids." He glanced over at Kay as he said this.

"Hmm!" she responded. May Ling took the sweater and looked it over carefully. "I don't know anything about knitting, but I know if something is old or not, and this is old. Go ahead, keep it. I'll add it to my report. Thanks for being upfront with me, kid. You have no idea how much that helps and means to me. You guys can go now. But I want you down at my office tomorrow morning at nine. Got it?"

They nodded, and Sean added, "Thank you."

A Questionable First Impression

It had been almost a week since Sean and Kay complied and met with Inspector Chan for their interview at the Central Police Station near Fisherman's Wharf. They had heard nothing since, and it was bothering Sean.

"I like her, she was nice enough, maybe too nice for a cop. I have this horrible, gut-wrenching feeling she simply doesn't have time for another murder, let alone one involving an old lady living alone whom no one knows anything about. This is San Francisco; she's probably dealing with a truckload of crimes, and most likely all of them homicides. I don't know," Sean said, sitting at the small, two-person bar in the apartment they shared in Sausalito.

"I know, right? My first impression was the same thing, she was too nice. We want a rabid bulldog on this case. I mean, she let you take that sweater. She should have arrested you on the spot," Kay said, trying to inject a touch of levity. "Which reminds me, Hon. You need to wash that thing. It has a hundred years or more of dirt, and God only knows what else is on it."

"Actually, I believe, well, what she told me, it's more like three hundred years old. She wasn't sure, it could be even older. But how could a sweater survive that long? I mean, really. We can't wash it; for God's sake, it will disintegrate." Her ploy had worked, as he was now toying with her.

Kay got up, heading to the bedroom, coffee in hand. She returned with the sweater. "For being so old, the wool is in great shape. We can wash it. It will be fine. I think, don't quote me on this, but it looks like hand-spun Shetland wool. Yeah, it will be fine. Come on, let's do it. I want you to wear it. Do it for

Seanmhair!" She headed over to the kitchen sink. After soaking and rinsing it out, she went to the closet where their stackable washer and dryer sat, with a load of clothes sitting in front that needed to be washed. She came back with a bottle of Woolite. "This is what my mom taught me to use. The stuff is pretty mild." She filled the sink with lukewarm water and added the soap. She held up the sweater, "You okay with this?" she asked, as she could see Sean cringing.

"I guess so. You know, I don't know the first thing about wool. Or cotton or anything to do with clothing. What I do know is I trust you."

"Ah, that was sweet." She held the dark tan sweater in her hands, examining the thick cables knitted, so they ran vertically down the front, back, and sleeves. The years of dirt embedded deeply into the knit made the relief appear overly thick, almost as if it were embossed. *That's going to look different when it washes out*, she thought, then immersed the sweater into the sink. She carefully moved it around to ensure it was completely under the water. "Okay, now we let it soak for a few minutes. Time for more coffee, don't you think?"

Sean leaned over the sink, mindful that this sweater represented his family heritage. It was all he had left. His mom and dad perished two years earlier, victims of a severe automobile accident, hit by a drunk truck driver. "Babe, I have you, and I have this sweater; that's it. Glad you know what you're doing. I might have thrown it in the washing machine and then the dryer."

Kay stared at him, horrified. "No, you wouldn't have. Would you?" she asked.

"Nah. Just kidding, I would have just worn it as is," he said and smiled at her.

"Oh my God! It's a good thing you have me to make sure

you don't look like a homeless man. Of course, then again, it's a good thing I have you to do all that techy computer stuff that's nonsense to me. I can knit or play cello for you, but don't ask me to cook or play video games." Kay giggled, then, after moving the sweater around some more, pulled it out to look at it. As she did, the water draining off back into the sink was nearly black. The sweater, on the other hand, was already a different color, more of an ivory. "Wow! Can you imagine the stories all of that dirt could tell?"

Sean looked in awe at the black water draining off the sweater. "Seanmhair told me this was most likely knit somewhere on some island in Ireland in the sixteenth century, maybe the fifteenth. So, yeah. There are some stories to be told by this sweater. I wish I knew the names and stories of all the people who wore it through the years. Be fun to research that. You know, Babe, I think I will. Research it that is."

Kay once again pulled the sweater out of the second wash and rinse. This time the water draining off was soapy but transparent. "I believe that's good enough." She rinsed it one more time in clear water, then asked, "Hand me two towels, would ya, Honey. We need to lay it on them so I can block it, after we squeeze it out. Which, important safety tip here, you don't ring out knitting. You have to squeeze the water out." As they finished, she laid the sweater on the dry towels, stretching and shaping it so that it looked normal. "Give it a couple of days, and you can take me out to dinner wearing it." Running her hand over the now much lighter-looking cables, she added, "Ya know, whoever knit this sweater was either really old or young and inexperienced. There are a lot of inconsistencies. Here, look at both sleeves. They're not exactly the same, lots of errors. I must assume, really old or someone just learning. But then again, knitting back then was probably pretty rough. So, ah, what about that dinner date?" she said, grinning proudly, looking over her washing.

"It wouldn't matter if it had been made by monkeys. It is the sole surviving piece of my heritage. I need to take care of it. Which, again, is why I'm so glad you love me. And dinner— deal, Babe."

Sean's phone rang, and, glancing at it, saw it was May Ling. "Hello, inspector. Any news?" Sean nodded several times, muttering "ah uh" and "okay," and then hung up.

"Well, did she find out anything?" Kay asked, fearing the answer.

Sean, holding the phone in his hand, had a serious look on his face. He looked up at Kay, "Yeah. There's been another murder that she believes is connected. In Oakland this time. A small bookstore. The owner was killed the same way as my Seanmhair. They believe he was tortured like someone wanted information. She didn't know anymore, just told me, told us to be very careful and keep our eyes open." His phone rang; again, it was May Ling. "Hello. Yes. No. No. What could my Seanmhair have had that anyone would want? She could barely pay all her bills. Okay, we will. Thank you. 'Bye."

Kay was standing close; her almond eyes, partially hidden by the bright blue hair sweeping across her face, were glued to Sean's. "What?"

"She wanted to know if I knew if Seanmhair had any antique books or papers that might have value. I told her she could barely pay her bills. You know, the only thing she has—" he sighed, "—had was a closet full of yarn and knitting magazines going back to the sixties. Weird, right?"

Cantankerous Katharine

Kay was not one to be denied her love of the crafts world, especially knitting. She convinced Sean it would be good for both of them to get out of the house after sitting around for a couple of days and to go to a large craft fair nearby at the Marin County Fair and Exposition grounds. It had not taken a great deal of convincing on her part, considering Sean enjoyed stepping out of his comfort zone for a little adventure away from his computer. Especially now, anything that would serve as a distraction was desirable. Besides, he enjoyed being anywhere with Kay.

They had been at the fair for almost an hour, stopping only for expensive cheap beer and organic vegan sandwiches because that was all they could find at the venue. While sitting on the brick edge of a landscaped retaining wall, Kay leaned in close to Sean and whispered that she thought there was someone following them. "Over there, to your left, to the side of the booth with the flags. The short Japanese guy in a white suit with sunglasses," she said, refraining from pointing.

"How do you know he is Japanese?" Sean asked while glancing to his left.

"Seriously? Oh my God, you really do think all Asians look alike, don't you?" she teased. "Chinese, Koreans, and Japanese are so easy to tell apart. Now, you redheaded, lily-white Europeans, you all look alike. Except for Tom Jones, that Welshman with those gorgeous blue eyes, curly black hair, and tan complexion," she said, pretending to swoon. "I could spot him from a mile away and listen to him sing all day."

"Whatever. But I did see the guy you're talking about.

You're right; he's creepy, looking like he walked off the set of a 'B' Japanese gangster movie. Though, really, I think we're both just being jumpy. Are you ready to head home?" Sean inquired.

"You're kidding, right? I saw a knitting booth earlier I want to go check out."

"Imagine that," he laughed and grabbed her hand. "Lead the way, my honey."

Kay pulled Sean toward a booth showcasing some amazing works of knitting, mostly contemporary versions of the Aran style, and shelves filled with hand-spun wool yarn. Beautiful and very expensive, but then again, this was Marin, California, where even the homeless were able to park their Volvos in their tent cities.

Kay picked up a set of whalebone knitting needles when a young woman approached. "Good afternoon. Those are pretty nice, aren't they?" the young woman said confidently. "I have some more over here that are hand-carved hardwood." She grabbed a set of black walnut needles and handed them to Kay.

Kay lit up seeing the elegant, almost ebony-looking needles. She held them up to Sean. "In case you were wondering what to get me for my birthday, Honey."

As Kay was coaching Sean, Elise Macdonald, the young sales clerk, was staring, mesmerized by Sean's sweater. "Excuse me, and I'll be right back." She returned with a spry but well-weathered older woman, holding her work-in-progress (WIP) of needles and yarn in one hand and a beer in the other. Her thick grey hair was pulled back, and she was wearing a faded, tie-dyed dress. Elise brought her over to Sean, holding her hand and pointing toward his sweater. Katharine's eyes shone brightly, and a smile came to her face. "Laddie, where did you get that jumper?" she asked, looking Sean squarely in the eyes. She then spat on the ground near Sean and wiped the chew spittle from her lips with her knitting. "Don't worry, Hon, it'll wash out," she said, laughing. Then took a sip of her beer.

Sean had watched the spit hit the ground near his foot and had recoiled slightly. He returned the old woman's gaze. "Yes, I've recently seen just how well things wash out of wool. Jumper, what is a jumper?" he asked.

"Ha, lads. You look Scottish, but you don't know Scottish ways. Yer jumper is a sweater, sweetie."

"I am. One hundred percent, but I've never been there. Top of my list though to go someday," he answered, then asked, "This sweater? Actually, my Seanmhair gave me this sweater––" he paused and sighed "––she told me it's been in my family for many generations. That it was my turn to take care of it. Why do you ask?"

The old lady once again spat in the dirt, wiped her lips, and took a sip of her beer. "So, you are Scottish then? Your Seanmhair, your grandmother. She was a knitter?"

Sean had moved closer to Kay to get further away from Katharine's imaginary spitting target. "Yes, I'm Scottish. And yes, my Seanmhair was a lifelong knitter. A very good one. Well, at least that's what Kay here tells me. Myself, I couldn't knit a potholder."

The old lady laughed at his joke and then once more ran through her spit-and-sip routine. "Do you know how old that jumper is? It's very old. Very unique patterns of clan cables. It's a guess, but I'll bet my granddaughter here's new boyfriend, that jumpers got to be two, maybe three hundred years old. It's a special one, laddie. You best do as your Seanmhair suggested and take very good care of it."

Sean smiled, "Thank you. Yeah, I know it's special. It is, after all, my family's heritage. I'm lucky as Kay here is an extreme knitter and knows how to take care of the sweater and me."

Kay laid the items she was holding on the counter and, looking at Kathrine, asked, "Can you tell us any history about these cable patterns? I know many of the clans developed their own unique patterns, so the wearer could be recognized if they were killed in battle or washed up on shore after drowning at sea."

Katharine spat one more time, wiping and taking a sip of beer before answering Kay in a more serious, foreboding tone, "I can't say for sure, but it reminds me of the styles from nearly thirteen generations ago when the Scots and what was left of their clans after the battle at Pinkie Cleugh, fled on foot then boats to the Aran Islands on the west coast of Ireland. There's an old wives' tale about one such clan burying their fortune in gold and jewels somewhere before they fled. Some years after arriving in Ireland, with their treasure hidden somewhere back in Scotland, they were nearly all executed by the English. The fable goes that the only ones to escape were a young lad and his lassie. The lad, who later disappeared for several years on a fishing expedition, returned to find his girlfriend missing. He was then found dead, washed up on the shore in Ireland, and recognized just as you said, because of the pattern on his jumper. The lassie, who was said to have the only map to where the fortune was buried, was never found. Rumors say that after learning her lover drowned, she fled to the New World with the map." She finished with a serious look and then burst into laughter. "It's an ole, ole story. A fable fer sure. But yer jumper is most certainly very ole and I'm sure has many stories to tell." She spat one more time and turned to head back inside but stopped, returning to look at Sean and Kay. Eyeing, the jumper offered, "If yer ever do get to Scotland, you should look up a distant relative of mine, Isabella MacDuff. She'd be living, I think, in Barrhead. She could tell you stories about sweaters like yours and how they were made."

The Large One

An orange hue peaked above the coastal range as dusk closed in on the fair. The vendors had pulled their vans and trailers up as close as they could to their individual booths. Elise was busy loading most of the heavy items into their Suburban when two men approached. Polite at first, they wanted to know about the couple she and Katharine had spoken to earlier. Katharine, busy packing things away in boxes, walked out to see who was talking to Elise. A woman who had seen a lot in her years recognized trouble when it was at the front door. "If you gentlemen don't mind, we need to get packed up. We have a long drive home. We also aren't real keen on talking about our customers to strangers." She spat out the last of her chew as she finished.

The smaller Japanese man looked first at his polished shoes to make sure it hadn't hit them, then turned his gaze back to the woman. "Listen, old woman. You will answer my questions so that neither of you should have an accident." He motioned to the heavy-set man accompanying him to stand next to Elise.

Kathrine grabbed one of the supports for their shelves and, wielding it in the air, fired back, "You and your bully friend don't scare me. Leave before you have an accident with this stick. Elise, call security."

Before she could respond, the smaller man produced a handgun waving it toward her. "Hiroto, stuff a rag in that girl's mouth, tie her up and throw her in their Suburban. You, old lady, keep quiet, or Hiroto here will snap her neck like a twig." Hiroto picked up a roll of duct tape and a box of supplies the ladies had been packing up and tore off a piece to cover Elise's mouth, then started to tape her hands behind her back.

Kathrine, not to be intimidated, swung and hit the big man with the pole. The small man responded by pistol-whipping Katharine, sending her to the ground, moaning in pain. "Shut up and get in the car, or I'll have Hiroto kill the little bitch."

Eye Of The Storm

The phone kept ringing. The two spent the evening out once they had left the craft fair and were doing their best to sleep in. Sean jumped out of bed to turn off both of their phones. But, as he started to climb back under the covers to seek the warmth of Kay's body, there was a loud knock on the door. With all of the recent events, Sean shot out of bed, looking for a weapon to take with him to the door. All he could find was an ancient Chinese Blunt Sword that belonged to Kay's family and hung in the living room. He approached the door standing only in his skivvies, wielding the sword in front of him. "Who is it?" he asked.

"Sean, it's Inspector Chan," was the response.

Sean slowly opened the door to see May Ling standing on his porch. Embarrassed, he opened the door further and motioned for her to come in. "Please have a seat while I go put on a robe or something."

May Ling, smiling, looked at him, "And just what the hell were you planning to do with a medieval sword while dressed in your underwear?" she said, laughing now, as she facetiously chided him. "Seriously, please go get dressed; we have had another attack, no one died, but it's bad, really bad. This shit keeps happening, and it keeps centering around you. Why is that?" she asked, then shook her head. "I know it's not you directly, but you sure seem to be the center, the eye of the storm. I need you to come with me. Is Kay here too?"

Sean disappeared to get dressed and returned with Kay, both wearing that look of; another *shoe is about to drop, huh?* "I need to ask you: were the two of you at a craft fair in Marin yesterday?"

Sean and Kay looked at each other, frightened by the connection. "Yes," Sean responded slowly and carefully, glancing back at Kay as he did. "Why?"

"Did you notice anything unusual? Any people who seemed out of place?"

Kay held her hand to her mouth. "Oh my God, yes. There was a small Japanese man in a white suit. He was wearing sunglasses, and I couldn't help but notice his shoes. They were the shiniest shoes I have ever seen. There was a second man with him. He was Japanese as well, but the man was big. I mean huge. He was wearing, well, it was like a tracksuit. You know, one of those shiny, polyester-like warmup suits with stripes on the pant legs and the arms of the jacket with a zipper. Oh, it said—it said—Nike on it. That struck me as odd as well because I thought *this guy has never run a day in his life.*"

"Thank you, Kay. Did the two of you visit a booth with a blonde-haired younger lady and an older woman who were selling knitting supplies?"

Again, Kay looked at Sean, the level of her fear rising with the realization of whom she was talking about and the story the older woman had conveyed to them. "Yes, we did speak with them. A cute young blonde lady who became very interested in the sweater Sean was wearing. Her grandmother, I think it was her grandmother, quite the character that one, came out to talk to us. She was quite entertaining and pointed out that Sean's sweater bore the markings of some old Aran cable patterns." Kay laughed, thinking about her spitting chew near Sean's feet, then realized this story, this visit was most likely not going to end well for the two ladies. "She went on to tell us of an old fable she knew from her childhood about a clan that buried their fortune fleeing the English army after some

30

big battle. And, something about a girl and a map. Are they okay, the two ladies, are they okay?" Kay asked, fearing the answer.

"No. No, the young lady is missing and the woman, her grandmother, Katharine Macdonald, was found in her vehicle near Stinson beach severely beaten. She's in the hospital's ICU, and I'm afraid in critical condition. I was able to talk to her. She confirms your description of the two Japanese men. They accosted her and her granddaughter as they were packing up for the evening." May Ling paused, slowly shaking her head back and forth, obviously carefully thinking about her next question. "Maybe you have some idea, any crazy wild ideas, why two murders, a kidnapping, and an old woman being beaten near to death all seem to revolve around the two of you? Well, you, in particular, Sean. Is there something maybe you have left out? Something I can use to figure out just what the hell is going on here?" she finished, raising her voice in frustration.

Sean could feel the panic rising as he stared at the floor. He finally looked up at May Ling. "I really have no idea who these people are or why they're somehow connected to me. I'm just a computer programmer, for God's sake. And, right now, I only know I want to do anything I can to help you catch them. They killed my Seanmhair. Why? She was a sweet innocent woman who never hurt anyone. Why? And that old lady at the fair, she was a character but as sweet as can be. They only sold knitting supplies." Sean was doing his best to keep the tears already welling up in his eyes from pouring down his face. He grabbed Kay's hands and, trembling, looked at the inspector, "I'm actually scared to death, May Ling."

"Yeah, kid, as you should be. Come on, I want to take

you to the hospital to see Katharine. She kept asking for you until I promised I would bring you there."

Sàbhail mo Elise

The drive to the hospital was uncomfortably silent. May Ling's mind continued the mental dialogue she had had since her first day on the job, wondering about the depravity of humans. How could anyone be so screwed up as to inflict such acts of violence on innocent people? How has our species survived when human beings can become so broken as to kill an old woman and an old man just living out their simple lives? How does someone reach a point of such depravity? Are they born that way, or does society find a way to nurture them, so they become psychopaths? The empathetic part of her nature was always at odds with the work she had to do. A tenacious inspector, May Ling also understood it was what kept her going. It kept her just above the line with the civilized human beings, just above the animals. *I'll get you, every one of you. You're mine!*

The light went from four to five with a chime, and the elevator door opened to the noisy bustle of the busy ICU floor. Just down the hall, an officer stood in front of a door they assumed was Katharine's room. May Ling held up her badge as the three of them entered the room. Kay gasped. Katharine was hooked up to an assortment of machines with tubes connected to her face and arms. Both of her eyes were black and blue with contusions on her nose and cheeks. Her head was bandaged, and her arms bore the marks of being handled severely. The watch nurse spoke quietly to May Ling, then left.

"She isn't doing very well, so the nurse asked us to keep this brief." May Ling said as she turned to face Katharine. But Katharine was already holding her hand up toward Sean, waving to him to come closer.

33

Kay, feeling an odd need to record the moment, took out her iPhone and started a video.

Sean drew close and leaned down, so he could hear her. She abruptly slid him to the side and, pulling off her mask, spit chew toward the floor. As she pulled her mask back on, Sean was able to see her rascally smile for a brief moment before tears welled up in her eyes, "They took my baby. They took my Elise. My baby." She cried as the tears started rolling down her cheeks. "They want some map. I don't know of any map. They want the map, or my baby will die. I'm an old woman; I have seen much. I know she's most likely already dead." She had to stop as she started coughing violently. Suddenly alarms were going off on several of the machines, and two nurses rushed into the room.

The first nurse to arrive started to pull Sean away so they could work. Katharine sat up, yanked her mask off, and, sitting up as much she could, yelled in a heavy Scottish brogue, "Sàbhail mo Elise, cuir am falach an ganzie agus marbh na h-uilebheistean sin." She took a final breath, collapsing back to the pillows. More alarms went off as the monitor went flatline.

~~~~~~~~~~

Sean and Kay sat surrounded by the dank, salty smells of seafood cooking in the open air and a hundred voices, all talking at the same time, trying to cook or order food. They found an empty table at the Wharf to sit and eat, which was unusual anytime in San Francisco. Sitting across from each other, they were both succumbing to paranoia, looking everywhere and at everyone. Their fear had become legitimate. Someone could very well be trying to kill them for something they did not have. Something, as far as they knew, that didn't exist. They huddled close across the table, sharing some clam chowder in a sourdough bread bowl.

"I have been racking my brain trying to remember all the stories my Seanmhair used to tell me about our family and where we hail from in Scotland. I don't ever remember hearing anything about a battle that killed almost everyone in the clan. I do know from my high school history class that there were many battles that ended poorly for the Scots and left the English empire to rule over them," Sean dipped a piece of the sourdough crust into the chowder.

Kay nodded. "Let's assume for the moment that Katharine's story about the girl and her lover or husband is true. That means there could, in fact, be a map. Or at least someone thinks there's a map that leads to a great fortune. That at least seems likely enough as a potential motive for someone to be murdering people. But why do they think your family, or more importantly, why *you* would have some old parchment paper map from the sixteenth century? If one did exist at some time, it would be dust by now. It's just absurd." Kay held out her hand, silently requesting the beer Sean held.

Sean passed it back to Kay as he simultaneously looked around at the people milling about. "Seanmhair really only talked about knitting. It was her life. You know that better than I do. She did talk about relatives we might have—ready for this—in Jamaica. One lady she told me about many times was not only a knitter but also a voodoo priestess. Cool, huh? Apparently, way, way back, eons ago, someone from our family sailed from Scotland to the West Indies and Jamaica, where he fell in love with a local girl who became pregnant. He sailed back to Scotland promising to return but never did."

"Well, there's a typical man for you." They both laughed for the first time in what felt like days." Kay passed back the bottle. "Do you know when that was?"

"Nope." Sean shook his head, then taking a sip of beer, added, "But, I do believe at home, I have the name of that lady, the voodoo priestess. It's written down in a book Seanmhair gave me."

"Maybe we should just disappear for a while, you know, and go there," Kay said, trying to be funny but thinking it wasn't a bad idea.

As Sean took another sip of their beer, his cell phone rang. He handed the beer to Kay, "There's still a sip left."

"Oh, fine, give me the backwash." Grinning, she took the last swig as Sean looked at his phone.

"It's Inspector Chan," he said, looking at Kay with concern. "Hello. We're at the Wharf eating and trying to keep a low profile. Okay. Okay." Sean held the phone, listening for some time, nodding to himself. "No way, really? What does any of this have to do with my Seanmhair or me? Okay. Okay, we will. 'Bye." He looked over at Kay, wearing a mask of confusion and fear.

"What? What did she say, Honey?"

"They have a lead. Another detective who deals with the Port of Oakland has been following two Japanese men, Itachi and Hiroto. They're part of the Asian Mafia who deal in bootleg Scotch."

"What does bootleg Scotch have to do with your Seanmhair or Katherine?

"You heard me; that's exactly what I asked. May Ling said they're somehow connected to a man by the name of Logan

Shaw, a Scotsman who's known as a high-profile criminal. They bootleg Scotch in countries all over the world. Apparently, the Japanese manufacture the Scotch in Korea. They bottle it using famous counterfeit labels and sell it mostly to third-world countries who in turn sell it to tourists in their duty-free shops."

"But what—what has this got to do with us? Why are they murdering people we love?"

"What she heard, but has no real evidence to back it up, is that Logan Shaw is looking for some important papers he believes were handed down through the generations in my family." Sean let out a strong exhale as he ran his fingers through his curly red hair.

Kay leaned closer to Sean on the table and whispered, "The map? It's real!"

"It would appear so, Honey. She also said in no uncertain terms that she believed our lives are in grave danger and that we should leave now, tonight, for points unknown. Lock up the house and leave. She asked me to keep in touch via text but to wait until we're wherever we decide to go.

"Jamaica?" Kay asked.

"Yup, Jamaica! That's exactly what was going through my head. How odd we were just talking about it. Who knows, maybe we can locate my relative there. We can just call it a vacation and try not to stand out. Let's go sit in the car, email our jobs about a death in the family, purchase tickets, then go home, grab our bags and leave tonight. I'm scared and kinda freaked out, Kay."

"Me too, Babe," she said as she turned one hundred and eighty degrees, completely scanning the Wharf. "Come on." She grabbed his hand, pulling him toward where they had parked.

Sean, a bit on the OCD side, had to clean up the table

and throw everything in a trash can twenty feet away, with Kay tugging on him the whole way.

"Are you nuts? You can leave a mess this one time, and I promise I won't tell anyone. Right now, the last thing I'm concerned about is how clean that table is or our jobs. I want you and I to still be alive!"

"Hey, maybe that lady, my relative, you know, the Voodoo priestess, can cast a spell on these assholes," Sean said as he turned from the trash can, trying his best to add some levity to the moment.

Too Close To Home

Standing at their front door, Sean brought the key up toward the door handle and noticed it was open, just a crack. Turning to Kay, he held his finger to his lips and, pointing toward the partially opened door, made the universal noise to be quiet, really quiet, right now, "Shhhh."

Kay's eyes widened, and she stepped back. Quietly, she grabbed Sean's arm and whispered, "Do you think someone is still in there?"

Sean shrugged his shoulders. "Do you have your pepper spray?" he asked.

Kay forged around in her purse and then produced the small glittery spray can. Instinctively, using her thumb, she rotated the lever to the on position and handed it to him. "Careful, I unlocked it," she whispered.

"Go back to the car and call May Ling. Tell her someone broke into our house. I'm going in to look around really quick."

"Are you fucking crazy? That's exactly how someone gets killed in every scary movie ever," she said in a louder whisper while tugging at his arm toward the car.

"That's slasher movies, and it's always the cute blond with big boobs. I'm good. One shot of this shit in their face, and they're done. Please, really, I'll be careful. Go call May Ling. We need to get our stuff and get out of here."

Kay, not liking his answer at all, slowly walked back down the walk and pulled her phone out. She stopped to call May Ling as she watched Sean enter the house.

Inside, Sean scanned their small living and dining room, which was littered with their belongings. Chairs were upside down, lamps on the floor, and every drawer had been pulled out and emptied. Forcing deep breaths to stay calm but shaking, he carefully made his way through all the rooms until he was sure whoever had been there was gone. He returned to the front door and signaled Kay to come in. "There's nobody here now. Let's get what we need and get the hell out of here."

Kay stood frozen, looking at the carnage in their home. She nodded. "May Ling is sending several cars over. I told her we won't be here by the time they arrive." She then went to the bedroom closet, pulled out both of their carry-on luggage bags, and tossed them on the disheveled bed that Sean always made first thing in the morning.

The two of them silently and indiscriminately grabbed clothes off the floor
and the bed. Kay stuffed hers in her bag. Sean folded each of his and then placed them in
his carry-on.

"Fuck!" Sean exclaimed, seeing his sweater crumbled up and on the floor. "That's going with us. I want to show it to my relative in Jamaica." He folded it up neatly and placed it in his bag.

Even their toiletries were scattered all over the bathroom floor. Zipping up his bag, Sean looked around. "We need our chargers for our laptops and phones. My laptop and phone are in the car. Yours?"

"In the car," she replied.

Grabbing the chargers, Sean did a final check and zip of both bags before dragging them to the front door. "Should we lock it?" he asked.

"Why? Let the police find it as we did. Let's just get out of here now. They might be watching us." She scanned the outside of their four-plex and across the street. Sean laid the bags in the trunk of their car and shut it as he, too, scanned the neighborhood.

In the driver's seat, he looked over at Kay as he buckled himself in. "Maybe it's not a horror movie, but it does feel like we're in some kind of true crime drama. And you know what? I really don't want to play." With that, he hit the gas, and they sped off toward San Francisco International Airport, where their first flight would take them to Las Vegas. Their second flight was the following day. They decided they could worry about where they would spend the night when they got there. Right now, their only priority was getting as far away from the Bay Area as quickly as they could.

Gonna' Need More Sunblock

Kay thought it best if they just stayed in the Las Vegas airport and took turns napping on the chairs. After all, she pointed out, "Here, we have all the food we need and the tightest security anywhere in the world." After a very long night and morning, they were able to board their flight to Jamaica with only one three-hour stop in Dallas, Texas. Finally, in the air to Jamaica and with no unusual or unsavory characters on board with them, they were able to relax enough to catch up on some much-needed sleep. Kay rested her head on Sean's shoulder and slept uninterrupted nearly the entire way.

At Sangster International airport in Montego Bay, refreshed from their naps and past customs, they caught a bus to Runaway Bay and the Bahia Principe Grand Jamaica, the only lodging Kay could find on such short notice. They paid far more than they wanted to, but Kay, the commonsensical one, figured they could better sort out any debts later if they were still alive.

Checked in and unpacked, they soon realized neither of them had stopped to consider what the climate would be like in Jamaica. They had no beach clothes. In fact, they had no tropical-type clothing at all. They were prepared for a foggy day in San Francisco, not the humid heat of Jamaica.

Dressed in the coolest clothing either of them could find, they made their first order of business shopping for something to wear. Something so they wouldn't stand out like tourists. They were doing pretty well until the sales clerk, just trying to be funny, said, "The two of you, mon, when you take all your clothes off down at da beach, you're going to blind people with your white skin. You're both whiter than the sand on Negril Beach."

"I'm sorry, these are nude beaches?" Kay asked, looking at Sean with a goofy, naughty smile.

"Oh yes, mon, Runaway Bay is world famous for its nude beaches." The salesman said, grinning at her revelation and response.

Sean, not saying anything, let his uncomfortable look speak for him. Learning just how good a salesman the young Jamaican man was, on his suggestion, they also purchased hats, sunglasses, and sunscreen before heading off to check out the beach.

"I always thought that being Chinese, I had the whitest milky white skin on the planet. Then I met you, and you make me look tan," she laughed. "The only color you have is your freckles."

"You're so funny, Kay, ha, ha, ha. What's odd, though, in your saying that, is I always thought the exact opposite. You're so milk white, so nearly transparent, that I look Latino next to you." Grinning as he said this, he kissed her. "But, you know what, your skin, pure white as the snow itself, has always been my favorite part of your looks. I love you," he added, then gave her another quick kiss.

"Ahhh, that was sweet. Tell you what: when we take all our clothes off, we can ask those walking by who is whiter."

"I'm not taking off my clothes. What are you crazy? In public?" Sean was horrified at the thought. "You can if you want, but I'm keeping mine on."

As they walked among many naked people sunning themselves, they finally found a comfortable spot that afforded some shade under a stand of palm trees. Without hesitation and catching Sean completely off guard, Kay stripped off all her clothes and then, handing Sean the sunblock, asked him to apply some on her back. Sean, still in long pants and a long-sleeved shirt of which he had at least rolled up the sleeves, obliged and rubbed the lotion on her shoulders and back.

Starting to feel hot and out of place with so many clothes on, he finally conceded and removed his shirt and pants, wearing only his slim-cut underwear, thinking to most, it would look like a Speedo.

Kay, having just pulled her knitting from her bag, the only thing covering her, sat it down and started laughing uncontrollably. "Honey, you're embarrassed. Don't be. No one on this beach has ever seen us before and will never see us again. Come on, take them off, and I will rub lotion on your back. And if you're lucky, elsewhere." She smiled that naughty smile again. Begrudgingly, Sean finally complied and stripped completely bare.

"You know, Babe, I gotta admit it, this feels pretty damn good in so many unusual ways. It's freeing," said Sean, sans everything but a straw hat and sunglasses. As he laid back on the hotel's towel, a man approached them from the FKK Strand nude beach side. Sean felt the wave of paranoia return, crashing over him like the waves pounding the beach. "Kay, not to scare you, but a man is walking toward us."

Kay looked up to see a handsome, well-built, and proportioned Jamaican man with beautiful black-as-the-night skin and shoulder-length dreadlocks. He smiled as he approached them. A smile highly intensified by near-perfect, brilliantly white teeth. Looking up as she lowered her knitting, Kay greeted him. "Good afternoon, can we help you?" she asked, trying to be both causal and polite while every muscle in her body was in flight or fight panic mode.

"No mon, I just came by to welcome you to our beach

here in Jamaica," he responded in a Rastafarian accent. "Nuh ta be rude, buh judging by your skin color, yuh both arrived laas nite ar todeh. An mi wud guess yuh both from Canada."

He grinned even more widely, exposing an amazing amount of white porcelain. "Mi name a Peter, buh mi fren dem call mi Pistachio." His accent put heavy emphasis on '*Pis— taaaa_chiooo*'

"Hi, Pistachio. What a cool name. Bet there's a story that goes with that. My name is Kay, and the redhead here is Sean." She paused for a second and added, "Wow, how did you know we were from Canada?"

Sean started to say something, then realized what she was doing. "Hi." Sean sat up enough to wave.

Pistachio sat down as he asked, "Do you mind if I join yuh? I know da area very well, and if yuh have any questions, I can answer dem. Also, if yuh want to know where to go in the evening for da best entertainment, I can help yuh with dat as well."

Kay, still on edge and a little concerned with his forward nature, said, "No, by all means, join us. We're actually looking for just a low-key vacation that includes lots of cold beer on the beach, knitting, some good meals, and getting to bed early. As you can imagine, we don't see the sun like this— ever. And we need to be careful how much time we spend in the sun. Neither of us gets tan, what with me being Chinese and Sean a Scotsman." As the words left her lips, she realized just how much the two of them stood out on this island. *Hmm, maybe we better work on our tans*, she thought.

Sean was thinking exactly the same thing. "Yup, we want to just toast ourselves a little, eat well, and relax. No adventures, please."

Pistachio had moved up closer to Kay, with his back

slightly to Sean. "Yuh cum tuh visit our nude beaches. Duh yuh both lakka tuh play?" he asked, giving Kay a wink.

"Well, no, like Sean just said. No adventure, no hikes, just relax. We worked very hard back home. Relaxing is how we play," she responded, missing his point until he started subtly fondling himself, clearly in her view but not Sean's.

"No mon, I don't mean tat kind of playin', I mean swinin'. Do you and your boyfriend like to swing?" he asked, grinning more if that were even possible.

Kay, clearly understanding his meaning now, said, "No! No, Pistachio, we are not swingers. We're not even nudists. We just happened on this beach and, well, as they say, when in Rome. Right, Sean?" she asked, trying to get him involved in the conversation.

Fondling himself to the point of erection, doing his best to elicit a positive sexual reaction from her, he asked, "So, mon, just to be clear, yuh nuh waan tuh play?"

"No! We are not swingers, and we don't want to play. Maybe you should look elsewhere, Pistachio," Kay said sternly, enough so that Sean was up asking, "Everything okay?"

Pistachio jumped up. "Oy mon, everythin' just fine, and mi haffi continue mi rounds. Eff yuh need anyting, yuh can fine mi dun at da beach almost every day. Goodbye." he said, and with his eyes already on his next target, walked away toward two ladies some twenty feet away.

"Okay, that was pretty strange. The guy is some kind of Rasta Beach gigolo. You know he picks up a woman or a couple, goes back to their hotel for sex, then tells them his sad story and how he needs cash."

"It's a way to make a living, I guess. This place has been hit pretty hard with hurricanes," Sean added, allowing his naturally empathetic nature to show itself.

Surprised by his mild response, Kay realized he hadn't seen the fondling or erection from his vantage point. "Well, it's at least better than a hitman showing up at the front door. Fuck! Can this get any weirder?"

Aloe Vera and Uber

Sean could barely walk. The skin behind his knees, right at the joint, glowed a painful red. His shoulders were a close second. Kay was rubbing aloe vera on the sunburned areas with one hand while surfing on her computer with the other, trying to find a lead that might help them locate Sean's relative in Jamaica.

"Oh my God, that hurts and feels so good at the same time. You know, Kay, Seanmhair said the lady was a knitter. Are there any knitting shops on the island?"

"A damn good idea, Honey. Surely, they would know most of the knitters on the island. I mean, how many can there be? The only thing they knit, really crochet, is slouchy beanies. Do you know any more about her? How old she is, any other jobs than a Voodoo priestess? Wow, what her resume must look like?" she said, trying to be funny, but somehow it all came out spooky and unnerving. "Well, looky here, will you?" She turned her laptop, so Sean could see it. Under the Google search, at the top of a handful of listings, was Choch ah Knitting. "I'm pretty sure that stands for *Church of Knitting*. It's in Browns Town, which is only a few miles away. Got a kind of a Voodoo ring to it. Wanna start there?"

The Uber let them off on a single-lane road lined with small shops, most of them obviously serving as homes as well. Choch ah Knitting, an old building, was brightly painted in salmon and yellow with green shutters that hung askew from the sides of the window a casualty of one too many hurricanes. Sitting in front were two chairs and a small table equally bright in color with several hand-carved wood statues and a ceramic skull sitting on it. Aside from a small sign sitting on the window ledge inside that read "Choch ah Knitting," there was very little else to distinguish it as a knitting shop. As they walked in, a small bell hanging off the doorjamb announced their arrival.

Kay looked around at a small collection of yarn and knitting supplies on the shelves painted yellow that lined two walls. A short woman, most likely in her mid-fifties, walked up to the glass-top counter filled with the many instruments of knitting. She approached them, smiling broadly. She was pretty, with dark auburn dreadlocks twisted so that some grey showed through and light brown skin with distinct freckles on her nose and cheeks. "Can mi help yuh ooman?" she said with a pleasant voice.

"Hello, we're not from the island—" Kay stopped as the woman let out a deep laugh.

"Nuh. Mi nebba wudda guessed dat," she said and laughed again. Kay joined her, chuckling.

"Yeah, that was a pretty dumb thing to say. We're looking for someone. A knitter," Kay explained before Sean spoke up.

"Hi, my name's Sean, and this beautiful lady with me is Kay. We're looking for a relative of mine whose origins are from Scotland. I know that it's a million-to-one shot, but we had to start somewhere. She would possibly know a woman named Mary Ellen Morrison, who was my Seanmhair, my grandmother, that is."

"Whoa deh boy. Mi kno well wah Seanmhair means," the woman said, looking at him curiously. "Wah mek yuh waan tuh fine dis person?"

"I'm sorry, I didn't understand that last question," Sean replied.

"Wah mek yuh waan tuh fine dis person?" she repeated

slowly.

"My Seanmhair said I should look her up if I ever went to Jamaica. That she might have some interesting stories about my heritage."

The woman again let out another deep laugh. "Interesting stories yuh seh. Mi boy, mi name is Agwe. Agwe Morrison. An yah mi kno yuh Seanmhair. How is shi?"

Sean was shocked. Here, at their first try, in front of him was his relative. The woman of whom his Seanmhair had spoken. His head drooped for a moment before looking back up into Agwe's eyes. "I'm sorry. She is no longer with us. She passed away only last week."

"Wah happen? Shi nuh dat old."

"Huh?" Sean asked, having a difficult time understanding the woman's thick Jamaican accent.

Kay understood. "No, she was not that old. And she was like a grandmother to me. She and I knitted together all the time."

Hearing she had passed last week, Agwe, a woman who had sharp, well-earned street smarts, had her suspicions aroused. "Yuh a ah knitter as well? Oh, gud yuh an mi will bi gud frens den. Duh da boy knit?" she laughed. "Whappen tuh da poor lady?

"No. No, I don't knit. I work with computers. And what happened to my Seanmhair is really why we're here." He stopped to take a deep breath. "She was murdered!"

Agwe's gasp was followed by silence for a moment. "Wah mek wud nobady waan tuh hurt dat dear old lady?"

Kay again understood perfectly what Agwe had asked. "We don't know. The police believe several men broke into her house looking for information. Information that apparently she didn't have, and so they murdered her."

"Kay and I believe they were looking for some kind of old treasure map from a story handed down over the years. We now fear whoever murdered her is after Kay and me. Somehow, they have it in their screwed-up heads that we have this non-existent old parchment map. So, we're hiding out and looking for answers, anything that will help us, help the police to catch the men who did this," Sean offered, doing his best to explain why they were there.

"Cum siddun. Wud yuh lakka ah beer?" Agwe asked, motioning to a table just beyond the doorway and the counter she used for business that led into her home.

"Thank you, Agwe. Don't mind if we do," Sean answered, grabbing Kay's hand and motioning with his head that they should follow her in.

"Agwe, I hope this is all solved soon. When it is, I want to come and learn everything you know about knitting," Kay expressed.

"Tab ih, strangle ih, rip out eh guts, dash ih aff ah cliff," Agwe said, smiling.

"Mary Ellen taught me that: 'Stab it, strangle it, rip out its guts, throw it off a cliff,'" Kay said, smiling and excited that she recognized the knitting saying.

"That's kind of a sick little nursery rhyme. What the hell does that mean?" inquired a shocked Sean.

"Silly, it's an old poem to remind us how to knit." She pulled from her knitting bag the WIP she brought with her because they were, after all, visiting a knitting store. She then proceeded to show Sean each of the four basic steps.

Agwe, grinned. "Yah gyal yuh a ah knitter an welcome eena mi kitchen any day." After opening three bottles pulled from the aging avocado-green refrigerator, she handed Kay and Sean each a beer, then sat with them. "It's interesting yuh mention ah treasure map. Ah story hav bin handed dun ova da years eena mi fambily as well. Eh did supposed tuh ave started many years ago wen ah young gyal fell eena luv wid ah Scottish sailor who did find im way tuh da shores ah Jamaica. Dem did hav ah little pickeney togedda. An da sailor wuse laas name be Morrison taught her how tuh knit as did is madda bac eena Scotland teach em."

Sean smiled, trying not to laugh. "I don't mean to be rude, but I did not understand any of that."

Kay slapped him slightly on the back of the head. "Silly, what are you deaf?" She laughed. "She basically said a sailor from Scotland landed here many years ago, got a young Jamaican girl pregnant, and taught her how to knit. And his name was Morrison."

Agwe grinned even more when Kay slapped Sean's head. "Guud fah yuh gyal keep yuh mon eena line."

It was then that Sean noticed that the freckles on Agwe's face were not from birth. They were instead a very ornate tattoo that looked like freckles but actually created a veil that ran from her temples to under her eyes and across her nose. On the bottom and sides, the pattern gradated to her natural, beautiful black skin. It was a skillfully done tattoo using black ink, only slightly darker than her skin color, making for a subtle work of art.

"What happened to the girl and the sailor?" Kay asked.

"Oh, he did tell har afta da baby did baan. Ah boy. Dat he did hav tuh guh bac tuh Scotland an wud return. He nebba did. Da gyal an da boy they be mi ancestors."

"And yours, Sean?" Kay added, looking at him questioningly.

"Would it be okay if we came back to visit you tomorrow?" Sean asked. "I have something I would like to show you."

"Bring dis fine knitting lady wid yuh an yuh a' ways welcome," Agwe responded with her wonderfully friendly grin.

~~~~~~~~~~

They returned to Choch ah Knitting the following morning using the same Uber driver in his less-than-new Ford Pinto with the front passenger seat removed to make it easier to get in and out of the back seat. Upon entering the shop, the bell once again rang to alert Agwe of someone's arrival.

"Gud mawnin yuh two luv birds. Cum eena," Agwe said, greeting them with her smile that lit the room. "Wah hab yuh brought mi yung man?"

"Wow, I'm starting to understand what you're saying," Sean replied as he held out the sweater his Seanmhair had given him. He laid it on the table, spreading it out and smoothing out the wrinkles. "My Seanmhair gave me this sweater. She told me it had been handed down for generations. I don't know why, but after our conversation yesterday, I wanted you to see it."

Kay, touching it, told her, "I washed it recently. It had a hundred years of dirt on it. The cables are subtler, and flatter now. I was thinking it was knit by someone very young who didn't know how to knit very well, or maybe someone very old who was having problems with their eyes or hands, or both."

"Oh, my," Agwe said as she leaned in close to run her hands across the rows of knitted yarn. She studied it carefully, grazing her fingers along much of the cable patterns. "Yah Dis a very hul. More dan ah hundred. Dis guh bac tuh ah time wen da Scottish still ruled dem lands. And Kay, dis nah da wuk addi yung ar da feeble. Dis a da wuk of ah good knitter. Deh a somtin bout da stitches. Buh dat nuh really dat peculiar fi Aran jumpers," she said, pointing to the rows of cables and continuing to rub the garment with gentle adoration. She could sense her heritage within this type of knitting.

A tall, handsome Jamaican man walked into the room. Kay stood up so fast the chair she was sitting in fell over backward. Sean looked at her, his eyes asking, *What's the matter?*

Kay, turning red, turned to right the chair. Then she returned her stare at Pistachio, the man from the beach, the Rastafarian beach gigolo. "Pistachio, correct?" she asked formally.

Pistachio's wide grin closed tight. "Oh mon. Eh a yuh both ah yuh fram da beach. Wah a yuh a duh here? Wah duh yuh want?" he asked, no longer using the English he spoke so clearly at the beach.

Agwe smacked the back of his head with a long whalebone knitting needle, "Petaar, wah mek yuh waah tuh bi rude tuh mi guests? Dis youthman a fambily."

Kay, putting the pieces together in her head, quickly tried to defuse the situation. "Pistachio met us at the beach the day we arrived. He offered his services," she said, shooting Pistachio a piercing glance. "I think there were some communication issues. And since you know why we're here, you have to know we were being very cautious. So, you are Agwe's son?" She asked half-smiling, half-grimacing at him.

"Ya ooman. She is my madda. I do apologize if there was any misunderstanding mon," he said, his English starting to return.

The little bell on the front door chimed, and Agwe got up to see who it was. Passing through the door to the front, the others could hear her greet whoever had shown up. "Gud aftanoon gentleman. How can mi help yuh?"

They could hear words being exchanged between two men and Agwe when suddenly Agwe was pushed through the door by Hiroto, the large Japanese man the size of a Sumo wrestler. Behind him, Itachi, smaller well-dressed, held a small handgun.

Hiroto held Agwe by her dreadlocks, pulling her head back. The smaller man looked at Sean. "You would be Sean Morrison, correct?" Before he could answer, Pistachio took two steps toward the man with the gun and, using a cross-over sidekick, knocked the man across the room, where he hit the wall, jarring the gun out of his hands as he slid to the floor. Pistachio then turned to block a strike from the guy who looked like *Odd Job* from the movie *Goldfinger*, then struck him with a roundhouse hand strike to the head. Hiroto dropped to the floor. Pistachio immediately jumped on his torso, preparing to drive his knuckles into his face when Hiroto powerfully sat up and twisted, grabbing Pistachio and dragging him off his chest. At that exact instant, Itachi, who had recovered enough to find his gun on the floor, fired a shot that missed Pistachio and hit the big man in the center of his chest. The startled look on his face didn't last as he closed his eyes and rolled over. Itachi jumped to his feet, walked over to Pistachio, and pointed the gun at him. They stared eye to eye. The smaller man smiled as he started to pull the trigger, but it was a second too slow. From behind him, Agwe stepped up and drove her sharp whalebone knitting needle deep into the back of his neck, sliding it up from the base of the skull until it stopped with a sickening thud as it hit the bone at the top. He wore a look of shock all the way to the floor, collapsing in slow motion.

Agwe withdrew her needle and stood over the dead man, shaking off the bloody whalebone needle onto his now-motionless chest, and told him, "Dat voodoo up clas an personal, yuh basssstard."

~~~~~~~~~

Pistachio closed the van doors and walked around to the driver's side to thank his two Jamaican friends. The three men had grown up together on the island. They went to school together, got in trouble with the police together on far too many occasions, and helped their community rebuild after the devastating hurricane. Today, nothing else needed to be said. They would take the two bodies a mile or more off the coast, weight them, and throw them overboard. They would also take the dead men's rental car to a local chop shop and make sure it would never be seen again.

Pistachio came back inside to go over everything one more time with Agwe, Kay, and Sean. The three were staying out in the front of the store, out of the kitchen where the two dead men had met their untimely demise.

"Dude, I still believe we need to call the police. No one on Earth is happier they're dead than me. They deserved it. In fact, I wish they had suffered. You, Agwe, we did nothing wrong; it was self-defense. But, if the police find out anything and come to talk to us, it's all going to look incredibly suspicious," Sean said, expressing his grave concern over Pistachio's actions. Kay, still wide-eyed and uncertain of the best course of action, hung on Sean's arm.

"Nuh mon. Mi kno yuh are rite. But the fact is, and mi cannot say dis enuff, there are several officers eena police department here, that are bad mon. Dem are criminals, mi kno firsthand. Dem very well cud be—no—they are the reason dem two mon kno where tuh fine us. If we go to the police, we will end up like dem, dead mon." Pistachio explained passionately.

"Honey, he's right. How else could they have found us so fast? I say we stick with the plan, and you, Agwe, and I go find a bar back near our hotel in Runaway Bay. We stay there until it gets dark and make sure we're noticed. Just in case, as you suggest, Pistachio, an alibi might be needed," Kay said, clearly understanding the possibility that the police could somehow be complicit.

Agwe was nodding, "Mi son a rite. Dem cops a crooked as ah dog's leg. An, for sum reason dem hab ah real bone tuh pick wid Petaar. Kay a rite let wi get to Runaway Bay an let Petaar an his frens clean up dis mess."

Sean was not comfortable with any of their plans and wanted to call May Ling to let her know what had happened. But Kay and Agwe were adamant that he shouldn't, that it was a bad idea.

Sitting at the bar, Kay was doing her best to keep a lively conversation going so they wouldn't look like three people who had just participated in the death of two men. She knew they needed to blend in, looking like happy tourists on vacation. Blend in, but still stand out enough to be noticed.

"I think it's time we consider changing our vacation plans, maybe head to Scotland to look up Katharine's relative, Isabella. I think that was her name. If it wasn't a secret to those two hitmen, then whoever hired them most likely knows our whereabouts," Sean said to Kay, which instantly returned the somber, scared look to their faces.

"Yah, yuh leave now is ah gud idea. Buh yuh need tuh tek Petaar wid yuh. He needs tuh nuh be here now. An as yuh si, he can provide protection on yuh lickkle adventure."

"Did she just suggest we take Pistachio with us?" Sean asked, his face questioningly contorted.

"Yah, mi did." Agwe said, giving Sean her authoritative, motherly look.

"I'm uncomfortable," Kay said, "based on everything that has happened but let's face it, the man did just save our lives. And he could well be getting in serious trouble if he stays here. We need to help him. My God, won't we stand out in Scotland; a Chinese chick with bright blue hair, a curly red-headed Scottish American, and a Rastafarian beach—." She stopped, not saying gigolo in front of Agwe, and she gave Sean a half-hearted smile.

"We'll be like the Three Musketeers," Sean optimistically suggested.

"You mean more like the Three Stooges," Kay fired back with a derisive smile.

~~~~~~~~~~

Standing outside at the airport terminal's drop-off area, Agwe pulled out three wooden dolls from her large knitting bag. They were hand-carved, hand-painted on polished wood, and decorated with seashells. "Dis a wah mi duh betta dan knitting. Dees a Nkisi voodoo dolls an dem will give yuh protection on yuh travels," she told them, handing one to each of them and kissing them on both cheeks. Then in perfect English, she said, "You be careful."

Best Be Moving Along, Again

The roar of the engines where they sat directly behind the wing made any conversation difficult. As the jet departed and climbed, Jamaica grew smaller and smaller, becoming just another emerald dot in the vastness of the blue-grey ocean, disappearing completely as they rose into the clouds. At 30,000 feet, the engine noise subsided, allowing Kay, who had been knitting since they boarded, to finally ask Pistachio about his nickname. Still knitting, she leaned against Sean, who was sandwiched between her and Pistachio, so she could talk.

He laughed, exposing his toothy smile. "Oh oomon, tat, is a story. Wen mi was jus ah little pickney, mi was wondering round a partay mi madda take me too. Mi saw people eating pistachios from ah bowl. Wen nuh one was looking, mi dug in eating handfuls of the nuts. Ting was nobody showed mi tat you were supposed to tek the shells aff. Mi loved the salty tayse and just chewed tru the shells. Needless tuh say, mi got quite the belly ache. An the next morning, well, let's just say mi was green and not very pretty." His laugh rolled out of him.

Sean smiled, "It's amazing that any of us survived childhood. I'm grateful to you and to your friends. Those men would have killed us. I'm pretty sure—no— I am sure they're the ones who killed my Seanmhair, so I don't feel any remorse. Fish food is a perfect ending for their sick, worthless lives. Where the hell did you learn to fight like that?"

"Oh mon, after high skool, mi met this amazing ooman. A bongo girl fram Merika. Mi was so in louv wid her mon. She was a karate instructor, a sensei. She taught ah vershun called Lima Lama that she learned living on the Samoan Islands. Mi was going to ah little college, and wen mi finished classes, she

60

made mi practice with her. She coud kick mi ass mon." Pistachio finished with a distant stare, remembering something—a time, a place.

"Damn, she must have been pretty good from what I witnessed. You're not together anymore?" Kay asked.

Pistachio went quiet for a moment. The smile left his face. "Mi luved her suh much. Mi miss her suh much. She was riding har scooter home from da store when ah drunk tourist hit her an kill her," he sighed. "Mi did nuh wan ta live nah more. Da only thing that kept mi going was mi desire tuh hurt every tourist on our island. Mi stole fram dem, broke in tuh their hotel rooms, dem cars. Mi blamed all of dem. Den it sort of became ah business, meeting ladies on da beach and convincing dem tuh take mi home so mi could tell them mi story and that mi needed money for my dying madda. Or rob dem if the opportunity arose." He stopped for a moment, looking at both Kay and Sean. "Mi sorry mon, yuh were just another set of tourists. Mi don't hate tourists nah muh, mi have grown past dat. Now, dey are ah legitimate way for mi tuh make money. Mi no longer steal fram them. It's bad for business."

Kay, already knowing the answer but acting astonished, asked, "Agwe is dying?"

"Oh no mon. She fine. Mi make dat up to sell mi story," Pistachio replied with a smirk.

"Hmm," Kay said lightly.

"Sorry, man, I'm really very sorry. I lost my parents to a drunk truck driver. I can't say I'm over it. I can't say I will ever get over it. I won't say I know how you feel, just that I understand," Sean offered.

"Wow. I'm sorry, too, Pistachio. We're not all bad, tourists, I mean. We all have families and people we love, and we're human and make stupid mistakes. Not an excuse, just a fact. I feel bad that the worst thing that I have to deal with, well before Mary Ellen was murdered, is that my parents are far too overprotective and demanding. They were born in China and moved to San Francisco before I was born. As I've gotten older and have heard so many stories like both of yours, I have come to realize just how lucky I am."

Out of the blue, Pistachio asked, "Sean, mi have a question. When yuh first did tell mi tuh pack. Yuh seh wi goin to Scotland tuh luk for yuh relative. Buh mi ticket seh wi are goin to Ireland instead ah Scotland. Why?"

"A good question," Sean said. "First, she's not my relative. She's a relative of the other lady murdered by those two scumbags. Kay and I thought about it, and assuming someone hired those two guys who are now fish bait, and again thank you to your buddies, it's likely someone is still following us. How? I have no idea. So, just in case, we'll land in Ireland, then take a ferry to Scotland that passes right by the Isle of Mann, which is just starting this season's Tourist Trophy Race. There will be lots of people traveling there, using the ferries. That should help us blend in a bit better. In fact, if anyone asks what you're doing there, tell them you're there for the motorcycle race," Sean added.

"Tourist Trophy race?" Kay asked

"Oh, yeah. For those of you who are motorcyclly race-challenged, that would be the Isle of Mann TT. Better known as the most dangerous racing event in the world. I wish we could make a stop there to watch the Isle of Mann TT."

"Oh, mon mi have seen videos ah dat race. Dem guys are out ah dem minds," Pistachio said, spreading his hands away from his head to indicate, *mind blown.*

"Sadly, we'll get close but go north up the coast, where

we can rent a car and keep our eyes open for anyone who might be tailing us. When we met Katharine at the fair, she told me that her cousin of sorts, Isabella MacDuff, would still be living in Barrhead, just outside of Glasgow. So that's our first destination, not the coolest race on earth," Sean said, feigning unhappiness over not being able to go to the race.

~~~~~~~~~

Everything was uneventful, exactly as they had hoped. The ride on the bus through Ireland, and the ferry ride from Ballycastle, through the Firth of Clyde and past the Isle of Arran, was spectacular but quiet. Pistachio, who had never been away from Jamaica, couldn't stop talking about how beautiful it was. Or how cold it was.

"Isle of Arran. Is dat weh dem mek sweaters like yuh, Sean?" Pistachio asked.

Kay spoke up. "Nope. A common mistake, one I've made myself. Aran sweaters, here they're called jumpers, came to be on the Aran Islands on the other side of Ireland."

"Good tuh kno," Pistachio said.

They landed in Ardrossan, where they rented a small car and headed toward Barrhead, taking Lochlibo Road and as many of the backroads as they could. At one point, they stopped near a large open area of the field being farmed where the River Garnock meandered through. They got out and walked about, making sure no one was following them.

Next, they stopped at a small pub on the outskirts of

Barrhead. Sitting in the car, they agreed to keep to themselves and not do anything that would make them stand out. All agreed that Sean, who at least looked Scottish, would ask the barkeep if they knew Isabella MacDuff. He would say that he was a relative from the States and that his Seanmhair had asked him to look in on her. With their plan in place, they walked into the aging wattle and daub building.

Inside, the room was dark, with low ceilings and a beautifully crafted wood bar. There were only a handful of people, mostly men and a couple of younger ladies, all at two tables pushed together near the windows. With Sean in the lead, they reached the bar where the barkeep was drying a pint glass.

"Whit kin ah git fur ye two 'n' th' lassie?" he asked in a very heavy Scottish brogue.

Unaware of beer choices in Scotland, Sean ordered the only one he was sure of "Three pints of Guinness, please."

"Aye, three heavies dis than. Ye'r nae fae thae bits. Americans na doubt." He grabbed three-pint glasses and took his time filling each to get just the right amount of head on each. Then he set them on the bar in front of Sean, wiping the bar with his towel where some foam had rolled off.

Seeing the beer's dark rich brown color, Pistachio looked at Sean and asked, "Wah da hell a dem man? Dem a as bongo as mi," in his equally not understandable Jamaican accent.

The barkeep looked at Sean. "Wat he ay?"

Sean looked at the barkeep. "I'm sorry. What did you say?"

"Da Rastaman wat id ay?" he said pointing to Pistachio.

"Nuh mon mi jus waan tuh kno wah kine ah beer a dat?" he said, pointing at the beer, confused by their mutual inability to communicate.

By now, all of the patrons sitting at the window had

stopped their conversations and were looking over at the three of them. Kay saw that their efforts to stay under the radar were having the opposite effect, so she jumped in. "Pistachio, those dark beers, they're Guinness beers, made in Ireland." Then turning to the barkeep, she explained slowly. "He is from Jamaica. They don't have any beer close to this. The best they can do is more like really bad Budweiser." She was clear enough to elicit a chuckle from the barkeep.

"Aye lassie, tell thaim if he cannae dram it, ah wull git him in ale," and gave her a wink.

"Thanks. Pistachio, he said if you don't enjoy the Guinness, he'll be glad to switch it out for an ale. A much lighter beer by their standards, but still heavier than anything on the Island," she finished smiling.

Pistachio's face lit up, and his smile lit the room. "Mi lakka dis guy!"

The barkeep understood that and, throwing the towel over his shoulder, offered up his fist for a fist bump.

Sean gave the barkeep his credit card, which showed his name as Morrison, of which the barkeep took note of.

"Yer had aall edy ald me yer ah Scot." He tapped the card to his head and smiled.

Sean saw this as a good time to ask him about Isabella. "Might you know an Isabella MacDuff? She's my Seanmhair's cousin, and she asked me to check up on her while we're here for the Isle of Mann race."

The barkeep nodded. "Aye, ah dae knu her. Her hame insae far fae 'ere. Her twin grandsons bide wi' her. 'N', ye'r 'ere fur th' Isle o' Mann? Thaim wee jimmies ur doolally."

Sean immediately turned to their translator, Kay. "I'm pretty sure he said her home is nearby, and she has twin grandsons that live with her. And the men who race at the Isle of Mann are crazy."

"Wow, how the hell did you get all of that? Can you ask him to maybe give us a map or a phone number?" Sean asked.

She got closer to the bar, turning on her flirt a little, and asked for a map. Without hesitating, he nodded and went to the back room, returning with a piece of paper on which he had scribbled a rough map, an address, and a phone number. Kay stood up on tiptoes and hugged him across the bar. When she slid down and turned around, the group of people at the tables all quickly turned back around, doing their best to pretend they were still talking. She smiled and motioned with her head for Sean and Pistachio to leave with her. Sean took the last gulp of his beer, as did Pistachio, who then gave the barkeep a double thumbs up.

As they exited the building, Kay looked at Sean. "'Don't stand out,' you said, 'that's the plan.'" Laughing heartily, they turned toward Pistachio. "And what happened to your almost perfect English in there?"

"Ya kno dat ah funny ting, wen he start talking with his heavy accent, mi jus turned mine up as well."

"Well, turn it back off, or I'll start speaking with a Chinese accent. And trust me, you won't understand a thing I say," she said, still laughing, and headed for the car.

~~~~~~~~~

Kay and Pistachio had done their best to convince Sean not to call Inspector Chan and fill her in on where they were and what happened to the two Japanese men chasing them. But what May Ling had told him the night he took the sweater from his Seanmhair's attic kept running through his head: how the truth would help her catch those who did this. He trusted her and wanted to help her find those responsible for the murders. He contemplated for some time what was the right thing to do, going back and forth—should he or shouldn't he? He wasn't afraid of the possible negative outcome for him. He would go to prison with a smile on his face for the deaths of the two Japanese hitmen. He just didn't want Kay, Pistachio, or Agwe to suffer for it. He decided, for the moment, it was best to leave out anything about two Japanese gangsters.

Standing outside their rental car parked at the pub, Sean walked about the property after dialing May Ling.

"Inspector, it's Sean Morrison. You asked me to keep you informed of where we were. Yes. Yes. Well, we were in Jamaica, but we're now in Scotland, looking for a relative of Katharine Macdonald. Yeah." He thought he had accomplished his task when May Ling told him she believed that the two Japanese men she had mentioned before were following them. That they were pretty sure they had followed them to Jamaica. She asked if they had run into them or seen them. Without thinking, he blurted out a half-truth.

"Wow, Inspector. We did hear about two Japanese men who were hassling some of the locals, and a fight broke out. Apparently, the local fishermen did not take kindly to their approach. The story we heard is that they're now shark bait. No, I haven't heard that name. Hmm, Logan Shaw? Nope. Wait, yes, I do remember. You told me about him. He's a bootlegger or something."

May Ling, so good at what she does, immediately felt there was more to his story. *I can follow up on that later*, she thought. She went on to explain that Logan Shaw was just the tip of an iceberg, that the bootlegging and counterfeiting operations included crime families in Scotland, England, Japan, and South Korea. That they're well-connected and have eyes and ears everywhere. And that they're extremely dangerous.

"Oh my God. Yeah. Yeah. Yes, don't worry; we'll keep our eyes open. Trust me, we're still freaked out and scared to death. I'll update you if anything new comes up or we change locations."

May Ling ended the conversation by telling Sean that she was going to share this information with a Japanese police detective assigned to find those responsible for the bootlegging and counterfeiting operation. She told Sean what the detective told her, *it was a blemish on the honor of the families in Japan who had worked so hard to maintain the integrity of producing Scotch Whisky in Japan.*

After she hung up, she yelled across her office, "Sergeant, get me the number for the police in Jamaica near Runaway Bay."

MacDuff Ranch

The map the barkeep had given Kay proved to be accurate and easy to follow. Things were finally going along smoothly. *A fine change,* thought Sean.

Sean and Kay were feeling a bit more comfortable, what with the murderers at the bottom of the ocean, the three of them safely in Scotland, and them closing in on Barrhead, which was near the home of Isabella MacDuff.

They were on a well-maintained dirt road, lined with tall old growth sweet chestnut trees, about five miles outside the town when they spotted, just as the map said they would, a sign in large green block letters, *MacDuff Ranch.* The Tudor house, another version of wattle and daub painted over with many layers of whitewash, was set back a quarter of a mile from the main dirt road. They pulled up and got out of the small rental car, glancing about. The nearest neighbor was so far away they couldn't make out if there was anyone even living there.

The three of them stood, stretching and scanning the surrounding countryside, feeling even better because of the remoteness of the place. Two young men approached, one with an odd-looking shovel, the other with a pitchfork. They didn't look menacing, but the tools they held told a different story.

"Aye, guid day tae ye a'. How might we be o' assitance tae ye?" the one with the pitchfork asked, smiling broadly, his curly blondish-red hair a near match to Sean's.

Sean stepped forward, holding out his hand. "Hi. My name is Sean Morrison. We knew a relative of yours in San Francisco, in the United States. She asked us to look you up if we ever came to Scotland. And, well, here we are. Do you know the name, Katharine Macdonald?" Sean asked, still holding out his hand.

James, the redhead with the pitchfork, grasped his hand firmly, giving a strong shake. "Aye, Katharine hud bin tae th' ranch years ago. I'm James."

It was then that Sean noticed these two young men were identical twins. If not for them carrying different tools, they would be impossible to tell apart. "Nice to meet you, James. Is your mom, Isabella here?"

"Na. Isabella wid be mah Seanmhair. Oor maw passed awa' years ago. Jack 'n' me we bide 'ere 'n' hulp oot wi' th' chores. Ye'r welcome tae come in. Isa is in th' scullery," James said. "'N' yer mukkers are?"

"Sorry. Mukkers?" Sean asked.

"Aye, lad, mukkers. Ye be sayin friends. I'd be Jack." Jack, who held the shovel, answered. Then held out his hand to shake as well.

"Hi, Jack. The, ah, band of merry misfits behind me, well, the beautiful young lady is my girlfriend, Kay, and the Rasta dude, who looks out of place anywhere but a reggae concert or Jamaica, is Pistachio. A pleasure to meet both of you."

Pistachio smiled and waved but didn't say anything for fear of another, communications incident like back at the bar. Kay also smiled and waved.

Inside, Jack and James led them to the kitchen where they found Isabella. A strong-looking woman, her faded red hair in a bun and wearing an apron, she appeared to have just stepped out of an Andrew Wyeth painting. Stirring something on an old Wedgewood stove that had been converted to gas, she turned to greet her guests.

Isabella was excited to hear these young people had

news about Katharine. As Isabella talked, Kay noticed she kept staring at Sean's sweater. Standing next to Sean, Kay rubbed her hand across the cable pattern on the front. "It's a pretty cool sweater, isn't it?" she asked, looking at Isabella. "We think it's really old and was knitted over in Ireland many years ago. Somewhere on the Aran Islands."

"Aye that is a fine jumper," she said, taking a step forward and running her fingers gently across the wool. Sean, knowing he had terrible news to tell Isabella, asked, "Can we sit down somewhere? I need to tell you something, and hopefully, you can help us with some questions."

Jack (Sean thought it was Jack but couldn't be sure because the twins had deposited their tools outside) pointed in the direction of the living room. They entered a room pungent with the smell of years of burning peat in the massive fireplace. Everyone sitting down except Sean.

Sean turned toward Isabella, who could already tell that she was going to hear bad news about Katharine. "Kay and I came to Scotland, and on the way, picked up our friend Pistachio—another story—because our lives are in danger, and we believe so is yours." He stopped to read the faces of Isabella and the twins. "I'm so sorry to have to tell you this. There is simply no good way to say this, but Katharine was murdered." Isabella gasped, bringing her hands to her mouth.

"My Seanmhair was murdered several days before Katharine, and a bookstore owner I didn't know but who also appears to be connected in some way. And Katharine's daughter, Elise, she was kidnapped and is still missing." Sean paused again and looked at Isabella, James, and Jack.

Jack got up and sat down next to Isabella, putting his arm around her. "How come? 'N', how come ur we in danger? Whit ur th' three o' ye involved? 'N', how come did ye bring it 'ere?" Jack said, going from showing compassion to expressing a rising degree of anger.

"I assure you, we did our best to make sure we brought nothing here. And we're not involved in anything of our choosing. Apparently, there is an old tale about a map that a young girl from my family brought with her to the United States before it was even the United States. A map that I was told may very well lead to the riches my ancestor's clan buried after the battle of what was it. Shit. Oh yeah, the battle of Pinkie Cleugh in the mid-fifteen hundreds. Katharine assured me it was just an old tale. Except for someone, actually a bunch of bootleggers, who were under the delusion that my Seanmhair had the map, then they thought maybe it was the bookstore owner or Katharine, and now Kay and me." He stopped to breathe, noticing the twins, and Isabella sat stunned and waiting for more. "We have no map! Kay and I fled the states to Jamaica, where I have relatives who are descendants of, apparently, the young girl's husband. Again, another long story. Pistachio here is a Morrison, as am I."

"Jamaica?" James asked, his eyes ablaze with hundreds of questions.

"Yeah, like I said, another long story. Anyway, two Japanese men, murderers, hitmen, assassins—whatever you want to call them—followed us to Jamaica. We think their job was to get us to turn over the map or beat out of us where it was. Luck was with us the day they found us. The two of them, the men whom we think murdered my Seanmhair and Katharine, well, they're now fish bait somewhere off the coast of Jamaica."

Slowly and deliberately, James asked, "Aye, then if they're as ye say fish bait, then how come ur we in danger?"

Kay finally spoke up. "An inspector back in San

Francisco, who's on the murder cases for Mary Ellen, the bookstore owner, and Katharine, informed us of a counterfeit Scotch and bootlegging operation that some pretty big crime syndicates run. A man named Logan Shaw, a member or leader of one of those organizations, apparently has reason to believe we have this fabled map. As Sean said, we don't. We don't even think it exists; if it did, it would be dust by now."

Isabella spoke softly but firmly, glancing toward Kay, "Please ca' me, Isa. 'N', ah have news fur ye lassie. Th' story o' th' map is true."

~~~~~~~~~~

Sean, Kay, and Pistachio looked at each other in complete disbelief. Isabella's affirmation was like seeing an apparition floating before their eyes; it couldn't have shaken them more. Kay pleaded with Isa to tell them more.

"Afore ah tell ye about th' map, as it's a lang story ah kin tell ye ower dinner, a'm needin' ye tae hulp James 'n' Jack wi' some chores. Sorry, bit this is a ranch 'n' oor problems dinnae mean a thing tae th' an aberdonian`s burd. Bit ah wull tell ye this, th' story haes bin tellt in mah fowk sin lang ago. That a young lass 'n' young jimmy o' th' Morrison clan did survive th' mass murder by th' English. 'N' that thay hud in thair possession a map created by th' elders that shows whaur th' clan's fortuin is buried. Mair a tell ye at supper. Aff tae yer chores, which, Sean, wull gie ye a greater appreciation fur th' workd that gone intae that jumper ye Seanmhair gave ye.

73

Furst th' an aberdonian's burd need tae be shorn. 'N' I'll have ye knu our aberdonian's burd ur native tan faced, identical as th' wool yer jumper is made o'. Then it needs tae be opened, washed 'n' leid oot tae freuch. Weel, ye wull see, there's wey more."

"I'm so sorry. Aberdeen birds. We're sheering the feathers off of birds?" Sean asked, knowing full well his assumption was not even close but had to ask.

James was laughing so hard he couldn't talk.

"Aberdonian's burd, ye wid ca' em sheep. We lea th' birds alone," Jack said, giving Sean a light smack to the shoulder.

Kay glowed with excitement at the thought she was about to learn, hands-on, the actual process of making wool. James had an odd smile as well, knowing exactly what was entailed. Pistachio and Sean gave each other a look of *what the hell are we in for?*

James handed out gloves and well-worn aprons to Sean, Kay, and Pistachio. "Follow me," he said as they walked over to the side of the barn.

Jack opened a small gate and brought what looked like an overinflated sheep into the barn. "Other than th' electric shears, Isa mak's us prepare her wools as her grandparents, 'n' thair grandparents taught thaim. It's solid wirk, bit rewarding. Thae days haun-dyed wool haes become very sought efter in tae industry. We even sell wool online noo." While holding the animal, Jack proceeded to quickly and deftly remove the sheep's wool coat in nearly two pieces. He finished cleaning it up and sent it scampering back into the pin with the others. He looked at the three of them. "Who's furst?" he asked, smiling.

Pistachio stepped forward. "Mi dun ah bit ah dat for mi

mada bac eena Jamaica. Shi ah very skilled knitter herself."

James cocked his head, not quite sure he understood Pistachio. "Damn ah, thought oor accent was tough. Ye maw knit th' auld fashioned wey?"

Jack brought over another of the overinflated animals, which Pistachio did not hesitate to start shearing. He was not anywhere near as fast as James, but he was still able to remove the coat in four large pieces.

"Nicely dane thare, Pistachio. Sean?" James asked.

Kay walked in front of Sean and took the shears. "You have no idea how long I have dreamed of doing this," she said.

"Most girls I grew up with wanted a pony, then a horse. No. My girlfriend wants her own sheep ranch," Sean tossed out sarcastically, looking at Jack.

"Better get used to it, computer nerd boy," she fired back at him.

It took Kay considerably longer, but with Jack's help, she was able to remove the wool from the animal, who was especially glad to get away and back into its pin.

"Jack, urr ye okay wi' helping Pistachio sheer th' lest six of th' aberdonian's burd?" James asked. "A'm waantin' tae tak' thae two ower tae git th' next batch o' wool intae th' pot."

"Aye, wi' this guy wull finish up shortly," Jack replied.

James took them over to a mowed field of heather where large clumps of wool were drying in the sun. He grabbed an armful and told them to do the same and follow him. "Furst we need tae throw this wool intae that pot. It's a mordant we uise that sets th' dye better oan th' wool," He smiled. "In th' old days, thay used piss tae fix th' dye."

He tossed his armload in and pulled his hands out. "Noo, ye wull be glad tae knu we uise a commercial mordant that is piss free." He laughed as he pointed to the pot they should toss their loads in as well. Once they had, he bent down and turned a valve, struck a match, and lit a fire under the pot.

"Okay then, th' ainlie ither fresh technology, is we uise a gas burner instead o' peat." He then grabbed a cheesecloth bag filled with leaves and berries and tossed it into the pot. "Th' dye. Kin ye gang gather up th' rest o' th' wool while ah keep an eye oan this?"

Isa sat with two flat boards with wire teeth that she put clumps of the dyed wool between, scraping them together, carding the wool as she hummed a song. As Isa worked, Kay had an idea of what she was doing but asked about the purpose of the combs and process anyway.

"Weel lassie, a'm combing oot th' yarn tae finger lengths so that it's ready fur whirlin'."

"You mean to spin the wool into yarn, right? And the song you're humming, it has a beautiful steady beat. What is it?" Kay asked, eager to learn everything this woman knew.

"Yer correct lassie. Depending oan whit a'm waantin' tae knit, th' thickness o' th' yarn depends oan howfur ah comb it oot." She gave Kay the look of a teacher explaining a math problem and wondering if the student understood. "Th' song. That's a waulking song. Come, let's gather yer two wee jimmies 'n' ah wull shaw ye whit th' waulking songs ur used fur."

Isa waved for Sean and Pistachio to join her and Kay on the back porch. It had been a long day for the three of them, who were not used to this type of physical labor. They were happy to join Kay and Isa at a long sturdy table with benches on either side.

"Yer lassie is a fast learner. So a'm aff tae teach her, 'n' ye wee jimmies th' purpose o' waulking th' cloth, 'n' th' songs we sing while doin it. We sing tae th' Scot's God, Loireag. Th' beat helps us tae shift th' cloth aboot properly tae tighten up th' knit. It mak's it stronger 'n' smirr proof. Bit mynd ye, don't ever repeat a song while waulking th' cloth. Th' spirits don't approve 'n' wull bring harm." Isa smiled as she arranged a large piece of material in front of them.

"Smirr proof?" Sean questioned.

"Aye, repeals th' rain." She used her fingers, moving them about as she brought her hand down to show it raining. "Veryone grab th' material lik' a'm. Noo wi' keep beat o' th' song, punllin it against th' buird, draw it towards ye then push it tae yer left," she said and demonstrated. Then she started singing loudly in a deep guttural voice.

> *"Th' aberdonian`s burd that gave th' wool,*
> *green th' pastures whaur thay fed,*
> *blue th' skies 'boon th' pool,*
> *where at noon thay made thair bed."*

Her voice and the beat made it easy for them to pick up the rhythm. Soon they were humming, pounding the table, and laughing as Isa sang.

> *"Sing th' back green o' th' sea,*
> *from wha's flowers we won th' dye.*
> *Sing o' sea-tang wild 'n' free,*
> *from oor misty Isle o' Skye."*

Isa had prepared supper for them earlier, and the house was filled with the aroma of stew bubbling away on her stove. They sat gathered around the large table as Isa gladly coddled over her guests, serving them bowl after bowl of stew and freshly baked bread. Kay, Sean, and Pistachio, especially Kay, couldn't stop talking about how they enjoyed the day's experiences. They all, including James and Jack, simultaneously leaned back in a sign of finished contentment.

Isa started picking up plates, and Kay jumped up. "Let me help you, Isa."

"No lassie, please sit in th' livin room. James grab th' boattle 'n' gie thaim each a taste o' th' golden nectar o' Scootland, 'n' uise oor best Glencarin set in th' gless cupboard. We have tae toast a dear departed mukker."

~~~~~~~~~~

Settled in, bellies full of fresh mutton stew with veggies from the garden, they raised their glasses in a toast to Katharine.

James stood, raising his glass high in the air, "From Robert Burns,

> 'Tae absent friends
> to they we have met.
> To they we have yit tae meet.
> To they wha have left us fur a while
> and tae they wha have left us forever
> let us hurl oor glasses.
> And dram a toast
> that thay kin abide in oor hearts
> forever."

As they all emptied their glasses, there was a knock on the door. After the incident in Jamaica, Kay, Sean, and Pistachio looked toward the door with grave concern.

Jack jumped up. "Who wid be stopping by this time o' night?"

He walked over and opened the door. A short Japanese man, well-dressed, bowed to Jack. Jack, not used to such a greeting but one who watched his share of Netflix, bowed back. "Guid forenicht sur, cani hulp ye?"

Kay, seeing he was Japanese, let out a loud gasp. Pistachio jumped up to head toward the door with Sean on his heels, picking up a poker from the fireplace as he went by. Seeing the commotion headed directly toward him, the Japanese man stepped back as Jack turned to put his hands up for them to stop.

"Whit haes gotten intae th' two o' ye?" he asked formidably.

"It was two Japanese men who murdered my Seanmhair and Katharine," Sean said, anger in his voice and the poker circling in the air. Pistachio, just behind him, was crouched in a dog stance, ready to attack.

The Japanese man spoke quickly, in English, with a mild Japanese accent. "Those are the men I'm after. I'm Detective Akio Tanaka. I'm on a case pursuing counta-fitters and bootleggers of Jah-Pahnese whisky, what you call Scotch. I need to find the two men you mentioned plus ah man named Logan Shaw," he finished, taking one more step back, recognizing the karate stance Pistachio had taken.

Sean lowered the poker. "Do you know Inspector Chan?" he asked.

"You must be Sean Morison, as it can't be either of you," he said, pointing to Jack and then James. "She would have told me you had a twin. Though you Scottish men with your curly red hair, white skin, rosy cheeks, and freckles ah rook the same to me." He chuckled.

Kay laughed out loud. "You don't have much of an accent, Akio."

"Yes, Inspector Chan and I have been working together on this case. She is the one who told me you were here in Scotland. She is very concerned for you, Sean. I am here onrly for information that will help me rocate the two Jah-Pahnese men Itachi and Hiroto, and Logan Shaw, who is Scottish." He bowed slightly toward Kay. "Thank you. I was born in Japan but went to college in California, where I also attended the police academy. The longer I'm back in Jah-Pan, the more my accent returns."

Sean stuck the pointed end of the poker into the well-worn hardwood floor and twisted it uncomfortably back and forth. "I think, by the way, you can stop looking for those two." He tried to smile, but it was more of a grimace.

Detective Tanaka relaxed as Pistachio stood up and resumed a normal stance. "Why would I not want to look for them anymore?" Akio asked, carefully choosing his words and pronouncing each syllable so as not to revert back to his accent.

"Jack, if it's okay with you, please invite this man in and pour him a glass of your, what did you call it, the Golden Nectar of Scotland? We have a lot to tell him."

From her seat, Kay said, loudly enough to be heard at the front door, "And we have a lot of questions for him."

They talked late into the night about the pride of the Japanese whisky industry. After the third round of Scotch, they were all mimicking Akio and bowing at everything said of interest. Akio spoke of how the Japanese revered and respected the originators of Scotch. He talked about how several crime syndicates from England, Japan, and South Korea were working together, overproducing whisky with cheap ingredients and bottling only months after the distilling process. They churned out alcohol that never saw the inside of an oak barrel. The bottles were affixed with counterfeit labels of the top Scottish distilleries and were sold in volume to third-world countries, who mostly sold the whisky in duty-free shops to unsuspecting tourists.

To Akio and his countrymen, the loss of income did not compare to the blight on the reputation and honor of the entire Scotch whisky community. They would not rest until they had apprehended all involved.

They also talked about what Akio's detectives had discovered, the information he had passed on to May Ling. They believed that Logan Shaw was in possession of a very old letter, discovered hidden behind an old painting made by a member of the Morrison family in the late nineteenth century. The letter, written by hand in Gaelic, was from a young girl named Ella Morrison to a relative in Scotland. It said that after her husband's body (that of Rory Morrison) was found washed up on the beach, beaten, and drowned, she fled to the New World with her son, James Morrison, to start a new life. The letter also stated that she had the map!

"This is why Logan Shaw or someone else above him, a possibility we cannot exclude, are after your family, Sean," Akio explained.

Finally, they talked about the half-truth Sean had already told May Ling. That two Japanese men fitting the descriptions of Itachi, which Akio told them means *weasel,* and Hiroto, which means *the large one*, had picked a fight while asking the wrong questions of some local fisherman. The fishermen, whom apparently nobody was able or willing to identify, took matters into their own hands when the gangsters threatened them with a gun. The men hadn't been seen since, but rumor had it that they'd been taken out to sea and fed to the bottom feeders. Akio's response was simple: "Sayonara assholes."

Not Quite the Knitting Lesson
She Hoped For

Kay was in heaven, dyeing, spinning, and learning new knitting stitches. Isa loved the attention as well because it had been a long time since she'd been able to share her knowledge with anyone. Her daughter, who had passed away, was the last to learn the ancient ways from her. James and Jack were helpful beyond words, and she loved them, but although she had tried to convince them knitting was a man's job as well, that fishermen had originally, likely invented knitting while working and repairing their sails, they were simply not into it. They spent their free time on social media and chasing the lassies in town at the various pubs.

This day found Kay on the porch alone, finally feeling comfortable that life was finally on track and moving along well, and, with the likes of Akio and May Ling on the job, they were no longer in the same danger.

James and Jack had taken Isa into town for a doctor's appointment, leaving Pistachio and Sean to tend to chores, and were up the hill mending fences they promised Isa they would do.

Taking a breather, Pistachio told Sean he was going back to the house for some water. As he got close enough to see the house, he saw two vehicles pulled up front. Sensing danger, he quickly ran toward the house, doing his best not to make any noise. At the side of the house, he was able to peek around the corner and see four men. One was tying Kay up, and another was taping her mouth closed. The third stood at the van with an AK-47. The fourth man, whom Pistachio assumed

83

was Logan Shaw because he was smartly dressed, finished writing a note and taped it to the front door. Pistachio took his phone from his pocket and started taking pictures of the men, the cars, and the license plates. As he took the last photo and started to put the phone in his pocket, the men wrestled a blindfolded, struggling, and muffled-screaming Kay toward the van. She shook the blindfold down and, for a brief second, made eye contact with Pistachio. He tried to convey, pointing his finger to his chest and then to her, that he would follow. But he wasn't sure if she understood or even saw as they stuffed her into the van and then sped off.

In disbelief of what had just happened, he ran to the door and read the note: *We will contact you here in 24 hours. Have the map or she dies. Do not call the police.* Pistachio ran back up the hill, screaming Sean's name. Before he got to Sean, he turned to watch where the vehicles were heading. He was still watching as Sean came running up.

"What?"

~~~~~~~~~~

Kay, blindfold replaced, tried to count the turns and stops they made, drawing a mental map in her head. She was surprised at how quickly they arrived at their apparent destination. This meant they were close, still in Barrhead somewhere. She heard the van door open, then someone grabbed her and dragged her out of the van. Holding her arm firmly, a man led her from the van. She could feel the gravel of a driveway and then the soft dirt of a path. Whoever was holding her stopped to listen to directions from another man. A man she presumed to be Logan Shaw. He told her captor to take her to the barn in the back and chain her up. "Use two locks," he said.

Half dragging and half shoving Kay, the man took her around back, where she walked through a puddle and could smell there were sheep nearby. He unlatched a door and swung it open. Inside, he took her blindfold off but not the tape covering her mouth. "Thare, sit thare," he said, pointing to a post that held up the loft above. She did as he told her, sitting down in a pile of musty hay that covered the floor.

The man, who was stout and wore a tweed coat and a tartan bunnet, picked up a chain attached to the post and proceeded to lock it to her right ankle with a leg shackle and then the left ankle as well. Once finished, and in an odd gesture of kindness, he gently pulled the tape off her mouth.

"Ye best keep quiet, or I'll tape yer trap up again," he said and left, shutting and latching the barn door. She carefully listened, noting he had only latched the door, not locked it. *Good!* she thought to herself.

"Hello?" came a voice from the shadows, which scared Kay so badly she jumped away from the post but reaching the end of her short chain, she fell hard to the ground, letting out a whelp of pain.

"Who's there? Where are you? Come out where I can see you," she demanded, even though she was in no position to be demanding anything from anybody.

A meek, scared, and tired voice answered, "My name is Elise, Elise Macdonald." As she spoke, she walked into the light, to the length of the chains binding her, only a few feet away from Kay.

"Elise Macdonald? Oh my God. You're the woman I met at the fair in Marin," Kay said, stunned. She was looking at a woman battered, bruised, obviously dehydrated, and starving.

"Yes, that was me. You were with a red-haired man wearing a very old sweater."

Kay stared at her, trying to mentally digest how this woman was there. She didn't even know that her grandmother was dead. Kay slowed her breathing, using a yoga technique, then responded, "Yes, Elise. My name is Kaylee Wu. But please, call me Kay. Sean, my boyfriend, was wearing the sweater. How on earth did you end up here?" she asked, still trying to fit the pieces together in her head.

"My grandma is dead, isn't she?" she asked Kay.

"Oh my God, Elise, I am so sorry. Yes, she passed away in the hospital. Sean and I were there. We promised her we would find you. But what the hell, you found us. How did you get here? Why on earth would they bring you to Scotland?"

"Scotland. That's where I am? That makes sense, judging, by the way, everyone talks here. It's all such a blur. I remember two Japanese men came to our booth while we were packing up. They kept demanding that we give them the map or tell them where it was. We didn't have a clue what they were talking about. Well, we knew the tale about the map my grandma told the two of you about. But grandma's a stubborn one and wasn't about to tell or give them anything. They started beating her, then started to beat me up to get her to talk. She spat on the short man and told him, 'You better take care of her; she's your ticket to getting the map.' That really pissed him off, and he beat her mercilessly. I knew she wouldn't survive. She sacrificed herself by saying that, hoping it would be enough for them to keep me alive. I guess it worked. They bound me, blindfolded me, and left me in a van, I think, at the airport. The next morning, they carried me onto a private jet, and, well, after several stops, we landed here. Scotland, eh? Funny, I always wanted to visit Scotland."

"When was the last time you ate or drank something?" Kay asked.

"I don't even know how long I've been here. There's a bucket over there with some really foul-tasting water in it. It's horrible. But I knew I had to drink it, so I have been. They've only been feeding me like every other day. The last time they brought me a plate was a day ago. It's always scraps from their dinner plates, and this time, they gave me a warm flat beer. Any other time, I would have vomited looking at it, but this time, I licked the damn plate clean. And that beer, it was the best beer I've ever had," she said with a smile. "I keep telling myself; I'm going to survive. I've been trying to catch a mouse, but they're too darned fast." Elise gave another little smile when Kay responded with an "Ew!"

Kay thought about it, mentally adding up the days in her head. "I think you've been here for at least two weeks, maybe a little less. You're right; it's all been a blur," Kay said as she rummaged around in her pocket, remembering that on the flight to Ireland, she'd saved some of the airline snacks. It was a habit she learned from her mother, who taught her the importance of being frugal and saving everything.

Kay first pulled out a set of short, metal-tipped circular knitting needles she used for making cuffs. She stuffed those back in her pocket, thinking to herself that she might be able to use them somehow, someway later. Then she found and handed Elise a small foil package of airline cookies. "It's not much, but it will help, I hope."

Elise kept saying, "No. No, I can't," but eventually grabbed the package, ripped it open, and devoured the cookies.

She started crying. "Thank you, Kay. Thank you."

~~~~~~~~~~

"Dem hab Kay. Dem tek Kay. Dem tied har up an tek har awey eena ah van!" Pistachio tried to explain. With the heightened distress of the kidnapping, Pistachio regressed to speaking in a heavier Jamaican accent.

"Slow down, Pistachio. I can't understand what you're telling me," Sean said, but deep within, he sensed that Kay was in danger.

"Logan Shaw kidnap Kay. Dem waan yuh to give dem the map in twenty-four hours ar dem kill har," Pistachio told him, doing his best to slow his speech down. "Mi will kill ollah dem."

"We need to call the police. Let's get down to the house. My phone is down there."

"Nuh. Nuh. Dem say nuh police! I took pictures of dem cars an mi watched weh dem goin'. Mi not think dem fur aweh," Pistachio explained.

"Okay, okay. No police. Isa and the twins should be home any minute. We can explain all of this to them and make a plan. Fuck, the map. I don't have a map, any map. Fuck, fuck, fuck!"

By the time they made it down to the house, Isa and the twins had returned and were unloading groceries. Isa took one look at Sean and Pistachio's faces and knew something terrible had happened. "Whit happened wee jimmies? Whaur is Kay?"

Pistachio handed her the handwritten note. Isa gasped as she sat down on the porch bench. Hearing the commotion, Jack and James came over and read the note. "Whin? How lang ago?" asked James.

"Jus before yuh get here. Yuh may ave even passed dem as they left. Here," Pistashio said, as he pulled out his phone and started showing them the photos.

James, who had been driving, nodded, "Aye. We did pass baith thar cars. Thay wur headed up toward th' highlan."

"Mi watched dem leave. I run up the hill an watched weh they headed. Cum, falla mi, I will show yuh," Pistachio said, tugging at James's shirt. They jogged up to where he had stopped to watch. He pointed to the spot where he lost sight of them.

"Ye did weel, Pistachio. Ah knu that area weel, 'n' that road ends juist a ways up. Thare ur only a few ranches up thare," James said, looking off in the distance and nodding.

"What do you think, police or no police? Because I sure don't have a map." Sean was trying to stay rational even though he was horrified by Kay's kidnapping.

"Na polis juist yet. Hing oan, ah might juist have something that wull wirk," Jack said and walked back to his room, returning after a couple of minutes holding an ornate wooden frame from which he was removing the backing and the glass. He set the frame and glass down against the wall and then held up what appeared to be a very old map, hand-drawn with words Sean was unable to read or decipher.

"You just happen to have an ancient Gaelic treasure map hanging in your room?" Sean asked, holding the map up and trying to read it. "This is the real thing, isn't it? Where on earth did you find this?"

"Bonny guid, isn't it? It's nae old at a'. It's a replica map fur Dungeons 'n' Dragons. Ah paid a bonny penny fur it," Jack said with a mischievous smile.

"Nice. It sure fooled me. It looks, feels, and even smells old. I assume that is Gaelic. What if one of them can read it and quickly sees the ruse?" Sean questioned, still studying the map.

"Ah hell, thay likelie ur gooin tae shoot us even if we have th' real map," James said sarcastically, but his wide-eyed expression gave away his fear of how close to the truth that might be.

"We kin set up a little ambush o' sorts o' oor own in case thay don't wantae haund Kay ower. We have some less than social mukkers wha kin hulp 'n' plenty o' guns. Bonny sure thay wull be glad tae hulp, don't ye gree, Jack?"

Pistachio, a seasoned con-man back in Jamaica, offered up an idea. "This map is good enuff tuh fool dem. Eff dem a willing tuh trade Kay for it, it will wuk. Wi jus need tuh package it so it luk even more lakka the real ting. See wi a going ta cut the battam off. Wi hand ova the top portion an tell dem they git the battam wen wi hab Kay."

Sean was just shaking his head back and forth, his brain overloaded as it went through everything that could go wrong. "This is all just fucking crazy!" he yelled. "I think we should call the police."

"Sean, if we ca' th' polis, thay wull knu 'n' ye wull ne'er see Kay alive again," James said, looking directly into Sean's eyes. He put a hand on his shoulder, "Aye, th' odds ur against us. Bit thay wull be expecting one o' two hings, th' polis, or us tae juist wither in fear 'n' haund ower th' map wi' no plan. Thay won't be expecting our bein' prepared. That at least gives us a chance. It won't break mah hert tae kill any o' those bastards."

No Map, No Plan, No Problem

"We have to figure out how to get out of here. If we don't, they're going to kill us! We're only alive as long as we have exchange value. Once they figure out there's no map, we're dead."

Elise, feeling minutely better with the morsel of food Kay provided, nodded. "I know. Every time he walks in here, I'm sure this is when he's going to put a bullet in my brain."

"How often does he come to check on you?" Kay asked, looking for a weakness they might be able to exploit. "And is it always the short guy who just brought me in here?"

"Two weeks... it seems like I've been in here for a couple of months," Elise said, shaking her head. "Yes, it's always been the same guy since they gave up slapping me around, trying to get me to tell them about the map they're so hell-bent on getting their hands on. I think his name is Bernard. His nickname is Bear. He comes in once every morning, late morning. I think they drink heavily at night and sleep in. In the evening, at dusk, he knocks on the door and yells at me to respond."

"Maybe I can get him to bring us some fresh water. We can't afford to get sick. If we can get out of here, do you think you can run or at least walk fast?" Kay asked.

"Girl, you figure out a way to get our sorry asses outside this barn; you just try and keep up."

"I love your spirit, Elise. You obviously got that from your grandma. I promise you, we're getting out of here, and you and I are going to visit her grave in San Francisco. Hey, how is your night vision?" A plan was starting to formulate in Kay's head.

91

"Not all that good without my contacts. But I can follow you or hold onto your shirt, and you can drag me. You won't lose me."

"Elise, I don't know if this will work. But here's what I'm thinking. And if you have any better ideas, please say so." Kay looked at Elise, hoping she did, in fact, have some brilliant plan to escape.

Instead, she shook her head, "No. I got nothing. I'm so scared I think the only thing I can do right is piss my pants."

"Yeah, I hear ya there, girl." Looking down, she shook her head. Then Kay reached into her pocket, retrieving the miniature circular knitting needles, and held them up. "Ever pick a lock?" she asked Elise.

Instantly, a Cheshire Cat grin appeared on her face. "Yes! When I was a Girl Scout, another girl and I learned how to pick all the locks at our camp with a paper clip. Let me see that."

Kay handed her the needles. Elise looked over the skinny metal needles carefully, then grabbing the lock closest to her that was attached to Kay's ankle; she started moving it around in the keyhole. *Click.* The lock's shackle popped up, and she swung it open. "Still got it," she grinned.

Kay was both astonished and excited. "How the hell? Never mind, this just might work. Can you close it without locking it?"

Elise turned the lock's shackle back and pushed it down slightly, but it wouldn't stay. "Think he would notice? I mean, he just knocks on the door and yells at me."

"I don't know. He has a new prisoner. He's never tried to mess with you or rape you, has he?" Kay asked.

"Oddly enough, no. Not once. He is either a gentleman crook, or he knows if he gets caught, his boss, pretty sure his name is Shaw, will kick his ass. Not that Shaw isn't capable of it as, well. For being ruthless assholes, they do seem to keep things strictly business. True professionals in a sick sort of way."

"Still, if we get caught with the locks undone, we're screwed in more ways than one. Why don't you try picking the rest of the locks to ensure that wasn't just a lucky first time?" Kay said, swinging her other leg over so Elise could reach the lock. Again, it was open in less than a minute. "Damn, girl, you're in the wrong business. Try both of yours. But do it with your eyes closed since it will be pitch black in here."

Elise had a tougher time on her locks because of the angle she had to work from and her eyes being closed. But, again, she opened one, then the other.

"Let's lock 'em all up again," Kay told her. "Tonight, when they fall asleep from drinking, we open the locks and look for a way out of here. I'm hoping there are some loose boards we might be able to squeeze through. If not, I might be able to get my arm through that gap in the boards on the door and reach the latch. We get outside, and first, we crawl so as not to make too much noise or be seen, then we walk, and then we run toward the city lights. Not a MacGyver, I know, but it just might work. We're dead anyway if we don't.

"A MacGyver? Like the guy on television?" Elise laughed.

~~~~~~~~~~

Their plan was hastily thought up and full of holes. But it was the only one they could think of on such short notice and after being up all night. It was simple: James and Jack, with rifles, would hide behind the large boulders surrounded by shrubbery. Two of their friends were already on their way over. They would hide down the driveway to prevent Shaw from leaving without turning Kay over. Sean, Pistachio, and Isa would sit on the porch as bait. The idea was basic and simple at best. When the kidnappers arrived, Sean would give them the Dungeons and Dragons map in an old leather pouch they found in the barn.

Once the men pulled the map out and saw it was missing the bottom quarter, Sean would demand Kay's release before handing over the rest of the map. After they produced Kay, Pistachio would walk out and grab her while Sean handed over the envelope with the missing section. If anything went awry, James and Jack were prepared to open fire. Isa as well had a pistol hidden in her apron. She had never killed anyone, but she had shot at and hit more than her share of predators on her property. A good aim; she wasn't afraid to use it now.

The twenty-four-hour time limit written on the note came and went. After an additional two hours passed, James, Jack, and their two buddies joined them back on the porch. Sean was inconsolable, sure at this point that Logan Shaw's henchman had murdered Kay. "We need to call the police. Right now!" Sean said vehemently, looking up. "That Akio guy, Detective Tanaka. We call him and have the police start looking."

Pistachio nodded. "It's time tuh call di police."

James nodding as well, took his cell phone out of his pocket, and called the police.

"Jack, go and fetch Bonnie, wull ye? Have her bring her things," Isabella instructed.

James looked at Sean and, leaning over quietly, told him, "Bonnie's a Druid witch, a very respected 'n' powerful witch. Maw haes utilized her services mair than oan one occasion."

~~~~~~~~~~

With their bodies pumped full of adrenaline, Kay and Elise had no problem staying awake after Bear knocked on the door and yelled. This time, however, he opened the door and looked in to make sure everything was as it should be. Kay thought to herself, *Crap, I'm glad we relocked them.*

They quietly talked over what they each thought would be the best direction to run. Both agreed that staying close to the road, so they could see where they were, was the best idea. They figured if there were any headlights, they could just jump in the bushes and lay down.

Hours passed. They tried to distract themselves by talking about Katharine and Mary Ellen and what great knitters they were. Then they spoke of opening a knitting shop in San Francisco together once this was all behind them.

Finally, the noise from the house abated, and most of the lights went out. They waited another hour or so, and then Elise once again successfully unlocked all four padlocks.

"I love you, girl. You're amazing," Kay told her.

They searched the back of the barn until they found a board loose enough that they could both squeeze out underneath it. Once outside and standing up, Kay grabbed

Elise's hand, hugged her, and then started carefully walking to the side of the barn so they could see the house. It was quiet and dark except for one interior light. Kay pointed to the car and van parked in the driveway that led to the road. Holding her finger up to her lips to signal Elise to be quiet and gently pulled Elise with her toward the vehicles.

They had passed both cars when there was a snap of a twig under Kay's foot. It wasn't loud, but it was loud enough to alert the two Dobermans sleeping on the porch. That there were even dogs on the property was a fact unknown to them, as the dogs stayed inside most of the time and were put out only at night for exactly this purpose, as an alarm. Both dogs started barking loudly and ran toward the sound. The house lights came on, and three men in their underwear armed with AK-47s and flashlights came out onto the porch.

Kay looked at Elise and yelled, "Run!"

They didn't get more than forty or fifty feet before the two dogs found their marks and dragged both girls to the ground, snarling and viciously biting their arms and legs. Bear ran up, and, shining his light on them, yelled something in German, at which point both dogs stopped, turned to walk to his side, and sat down.

Bad To Worse

Later in the evening (much later than anyone should normally be knocking on a door), Detective Akio Tanaka and another police officer were there, knocking. James opened the door and knew instantly that this was not going to be good. "Detective, come in, baith o' ye." He opened the door wider, so both could enter. But instead of walking over to where everyone was seated, the men stood in the entryway.

"Evening. This is DCI Ferguson. He's from the Strathclyde Police in Glasgow," Akio said, formally introducing the officer. "I'll let him explain why we're here," he said, turning to the older policeman.

"Sorry tae baather ye folks at this late oor, bit Akio assured me this might be relevant." Years of experience had taught him not to beat around the bush. He told his men that when you have something tough to tell someone, get to it; just *put a bullet through the brain*. Don't let them have a chance to think about it. "We have a female body that was foun this mornin' at a micro-distillery jist ootside Glasgow."

Sean's heart went straight to his throat, "NO! Noooooo, it can't be."

Pistachio felt his entire body go limp, his head and shoulders slumping but was still able to offer, "Hear him out. Wi nuh kno dat Kay."

"A'm sorry. Th' young jimmy is correct. We need ye tae come wi' us tae th' distillery tae see if ye kin identify th' body afore it's moved."

Sean suddenly felt the need to vomit but didn't. He stood up, turning to DCI Ferguson.

"I understand." He took a huge breath. "I need to know

as well."

Pistachio stood up, "A goin tu," he said, knowing his friend, Sean, was dying inside.

It was a somber thirty-minute drive to the Simpson & Shaw Distillery set against a backdrop of highland peaks and the night's array of stars with a hint of the Milky Way's spiral arms appearing like streaks of fog. DCI Ferguson led them toward the distillery's front door and then under the yellow tape. As a formality, he showed the officer guarding the entrance his badge. Crossing once again under the yellow tape, for the second time in less than a month, Sean felt his mind reel as he went over the five recent deaths he was somehow at the center of. And now, Kay. He stopped, putting his arm on Pistachio. "I'm not sure I can do this."

"Mi get yuh mon. Yuh can duh dis. Yuh haffta duh dis."

DCI Ferguson led them through a gift shop and bar and into a large room filled with copper pot stills. He pushed through a set of doors into the room housing the malting floor, still covered with a layer of barley, with wooden shovels lining the brick wall. The air was filled with the pungent smell of the germinating, barely converting to malt. It would be intoxicating under any other circumstances, but not tonight. Finally, they made their way into the kiln room, which was decorated with a high pagoda ceiling.

In the middle of the room was a rotary drum kiln fed by a brick furnace. The kiln's peat fire now extinguished, they walked over to the drum's open hatch. Sean walked to the drum with his head down, then paused; he took a deep breath and looked in. He flinched, not at all prepared for how badly the body was burned and disfigured after rotating in the drum for hours. He took a step back, turned, and vomited onto the concrete floor.

Putting his hand lightly on his back, Detective Akio asked, "You okay, Sean?"

Sean righted himself, wiping his mouth and face with his sleeve. "No. But I'll be okay. I can't tell who that is. But you know what? My instinct, the way I feel when I'm around Kay, says that's not her. I just don't know. I can't give you an answer."

Pistachio glanced in and immediately turned away. "Let's git outta here. Wah wud yuh even bring us here? Nuh one can tell wuu dat is."

"C'moan," DCI Ferguson told them, "follow me. I'm sorry. Ah pure am. Bit, if thare is ony chance o' finding yer mukker, we hae tae pursue ilka leid, ilka clue. Na maiter howfur difficult. I'll take the motor ye back. Saergent tell forensics thay kin remove th' body 'n' tak' it tae th' yard."

They headed back to the MacDuff ranch as the moonlight broke through the trees pouring out onto the road creating an eerie ambiance that only added to the night's dread. Sean recovered enough to ask, "That person, that woman—I refuse to believe that's Kay—did they burn her to death in that kiln?"

"Na, th' coroner oan th' scene haes awready discover th' cause o' death. She was mercifully shot in th' heid afore bein' tossed intae th' kiln. A'm waantin' this one wha did this. A'm waantin' him baad."

Sean sat back on the rear seat, fuming. "If that is Kay, what was she doing in that distillery? Why? What is the matter with these animals? If it's her, I will kill every last one of them if it takes me the rest of my life."

"We knoo nothing at this point. How come whoever that was, was thare, is a mystery. But, it's a lead fur us. We knoo one o' th' owners o' this distillery is Logan Shaw, a jimmy detective Akio 'ere haes bin follaein. This is a' tied intae a bootlegging operation that involves loads of muckle crime syndicates. 'N' aye, they're heartless bastards who don't deserve tae breath th' same air. Bit laddie, dae be careful wi' statements lik' tat. Thay kin come back tae bite ye in th' bahookie.

Sean nodded. "Don't know what a bahookie is, but I get the drift. Sorry."

"Nuh need tuh bi sorry mon. Eff dat was Kay mi will help yuh fine an kill dem," Pistachio told him.

"Whin we git tae yer hoose, dae ye have ony personal belongs we kin uise tae git Kay's DNA? A toothbrush, hairbrush, clothing she wore recently that haes nae bin washed?"

"Yeah, I can get you something. How long will it take before we know?" he asked as he got out of the car.

"Th' guys at Scootlund Yaird ur bonny fleet. Twenty-four tae seventy-two hours," he said, as Sean walked toward the house in a daze. Inside, he grabbed her hairbrush from her daypack.

Returning, he dropped the brush into a plastic bag the officer had opened up. "Thanks, son. As soon as I hear, ah wull let Detective Tanaka knoo."

~~~~~~~~~~

Two nights later, the sound of another knock on the door, once again late in the evening, filled the house with foreboding and apprehension. James opened the door, prepared for the worst. He was sure this would be news of a positive DNA match. Instead, there stood a short Asian woman with cropped black hair. Behind her was Detective Tanaka.

Temporarily caught off guard, he stared at her until he recognized Akio behind her. "Detective Tanaka, ye 'n' yer mukker come in, please."

"Jack, this is Inspector May Ling Chan from San Francisco. She is aquatinted with Sean and this case."

"Good evening, Jack," she said, offering her hand.

James shook her hand and said, "I'm James. Jack is inside." He waved them both in toward the living room where Isabella, Jack, Sean, and Pistachio sat in front of a comfortably smoldering peat fire. Sean jumped up to hug May Ling. "Oh my God, May Ling. Why are you here?" Sean asked, concern written all over *his face. If May Ling is here*, he thought, *she must know something terrible has happened to Kay.*

May Ling wrapped her arms around Sean. "I don't know what it is about you two. But for some reason—" she paused. "—you know, I'm never supposed to allow myself to become emotionally attached to the people in a case. But I love you two. When I heard Kay had been kidnapped and Akio here called me about the unidentified girl they feared could be Kay, I left my beautiful Soomee still lying in a warm bed in the middle of the night. The second time mind you. And hopped the next flight here." She hugged Sean even tighter.

Akio, squinting, looked at May Ling, "Isn't Soomee your Medical Examiner?" he asked.

May Ling answered with a slightly coy smile. "Yes. Soomee and I have been together for just over a year now."

"Does not your department have strict rures against fraternizing with other department members?" Akio asked.

101

Sean spoke before she could answer. "Kay and I met Soomee when we came to the interview. She's beautiful. That's awesome. I think you two are perfect for each other. Screw the rules." Then looking down in despair, he asked, "But if you're here, is there something you need to tell me about Kay? God, I miss her, and I'm so scared."

May Ling looked first at Detective Tanaka and held her finger to her lips. "Yes. Shh." Then turning to meet Sean's questioning stare, she responded, "No, Sean. I have no new information. I'm here to help you find her and the bastards who murdered your gran—sorry, your Seanmhair, Kathrine, and kidnapped her daughter. I told you I wouldn't rest until I get them. And I won't! How are you holding up, Sean?" She asked.

"Oh, just dandy," he scoffed. "Seriously, May Ling, I'm a total wreck. Has either of you heard from forensics? Do they know anything yet?"

Akio spoke, walking into the flickering light of the fire. "No. I called an hour ago, and they still have nothing. Sorry."

Isabella got up. "Kin ah git ony o' ye a heavy?" she asked.

May Ling, unfamiliar with the term, had to ask, "A heavy?"

Pistachio said, with a somber chuckle, "An everyone tinks mia haad to undastan."

"I can't understand any of them, May Ling. Sorry, Inspector. A heavy, I have come to learn, is a pint of beer," Sean explained.

"Sean, you and I have been through enough that you can dispense with the inspector shit. Call me May or May Ling. And this—" she said, pointing toward Pistachio, "—must be Peter, or Pistachio, Agwe Morrison's son?"

"Ya nuh mi mada?" Pistachio asked, looking at her with

cautious reservation.

"Let's just say I've been looking into the disappearance of my two prime suspects since your new friends, Sean and Kay arrived in Jamaica and met you."

Pistachio tried not to but ended up turning to look at Sean.

"Yes, I know you and your mother are Sean's distant relatives," May Ling said, looking keenly into Pistachio's eyes. "And yes, ma'am," turning to Isa, "I would love a beer. It was a very long flight with only snacks and water."

"Please, ca' me Isa. I'll bring ye baith a heavy 'n' something tae sloch."

"Sloch? Never mind, I think I got it. Thank you, Isa."

Akio nodded, grinning, stifling the laugh he knew was inappropriate in a room heavy with despair. "Yes, Isa, a heavy for me as well. Thank you."

You Can Feel the Evil

Pistachio picked up his cell phone, surprised that anyone would call him while he was in Scotland. Or, that an old phone with a local Jamaican provider would even get reception. It was Agwe.

"Petaar. Everyting ah rie?" she blurted out for a greeting. "Mi can feel ih tru contagion contact. Mi saved items fram ah each ah yuh. An mi feel serious evil surrounding Kay. Wah hav happened?"

Pistachio walked over to where Sean was taking a break from Isa's chores and was leaning on a fence post. As he did, Pistachio put his phone on speaker. "It's mi mada. Shi a worry bout Kay. Shi say shi can feel somtin is wrong."

"Hi, Agwe, this is Sean. You're on speakerphone. I'm afraid your feelings are correct. Kay was kidnapped by the men who hired those two Japanese men. We were supposed to do a trade with them—the map for Kay, but they never showed up. Agwe, I have the most God-awful feeling."

"Oh nuh. Kay still alive. Mi sense har spirit. Shi a ah strong one dat pickney," Agwe told Sean. "Da mon huu kidnapped har a very evil. Mia goin tae increase da protection spells mi hab areddi put on da dolls. An mi goin sen dem sum very evil spirits tuh contend with. Si how da lakka facing real evil."

"I appreciate that, Agwe. But right now, we need the police working on this. We have an idea of where they might be holding Kay captive. We've told the police, and they are working on it." Sean answered Agwe, allowing his disbelief in magic to show.

Sensing his misgivings, she explained, "Mi spent much

ah my yuth eena Haiti wid mi mada an stepdad. Afta many years mi Lakou granted mi da title ah Priestess an did ask mi tuh return tuh Jamaica tuh spread da word. It's real enough, Sean. Mi taak tuh da spirits between worlds often," Agwe said, doing her best to educate Sean and quell his fear of magic and voodoo. "Petaar did tell mi bout yuh Druid Witch frend. She will tell yuh. Deh a lickkle difference eena wah wi duh. Wi both channel spirits tuh help us. Dem all da same spirits. Wi hab jus give dem difrent names bikaaz of our histories an of our languages. Mi welcome Isabella's help. Har Druid Witch frend, Bonnie, shi will be ah powerful ally—" Pistachio turned, changing his position next to Sean, and the call dropped.

"Sorry, dis cell really shud not even wuk over here. But shi a tellin the truth Sean. Da spirit wurld is real an' very powerful."

An Elevated View

With Jack following him, James approached Pistachio and Sean. James was carrying a gray plastic suitcase, which he sat on the ground. Looking up at both of them, he asked, "Wantae goin tak' a peek at th' hoose up th' hill?"
As he spoke, he opened the suitcase and pulled back the cover to expose an expensive-looking drone and controller, and all tucked neatly into its form-fitting foam padding.

Sean's spirits instantly rose. "Oh my God, yes! Can you control it this far away, or do we need to get closer?"

Pistachio was already on his hands and knees, looking at the amazing technology he knew of but had never seen. "Oh mon, this is cool!"

"Aye, we can motor up th' road tae whaur it ends juist past whaur th' hoose is. We kin watch 'n' record th' entire flight wi'," he said, pulling out the controller and handing it to Sean.

"What the hell are we standing around here for? Let's go." Sean put up his hand to say no to holding the controller, then turning back toward the fence, he leaned the shovel he had been using against a post and headed for the car. "Come on," he said, waving them on.

James's half smile said it all as he patted his brother on the back, "Guid ca', Jack."

"Can't hurt. Who knos whit we wull discover? Keep it up high so thay can't 'ere it or see it," he reminded his brother. "He's right, let's dae this."

They parked the car in a wooded area, so it wouldn't be seen from the road were someone to approach. Then, they bushwhacked through the knee-high grass and brush to a large rock outcrop with sufficient cover they could hide behind. Jack watched below with his binoculars while James readied the drone.

"Na movement at a'. Thare ur two cars 'n' a van parked up near th' hoose," Jack reported.

The drone lifted off and went straight up into the air. As he worked to get it high enough, they could barely see it or hear it. Then with James, Sean, and Pistachio all huddled close enough to view the small screen, he flew it toward the house. From above, it was as Jack described: void of movement. He circled the house, zooming the camera in on the porch and the cars. Nothing. After fifteen minutes in the air and seeing no signs to indicate someone was being held hostage, James feeling dejected looked at them and said, "Ah think that's it. Mibbie we kin come back at dusk 'n'—"

"Nuh. Deh, look there people a cum outta da bac of the house," Pistachio interrupted excitedly.

The three almost hit heads looking back at the tiny screen again. They watched as two men wearing tweed blazers steered a woman with bright blue hair and hands bound behind her toward a barn.

"That's Kay! Oh my God, that's Kay. Agwe was right, Pistachio," Sean said, his emotions pouring out of him in tears. "She's alive. We need to get this video to the police. We need to call May Ling."

"Git dat drone outta there before anyone sees it," Pistachio suggested, an earnest pleading in his voice.

Jack crawled back to where they were at the rock and shook his head, "Na. Goo higher bit don't shift it horizontally 'til thay reach th' barn. Thay might see it if ye shift o'er th' sky." As Jack explained, James nodded. They waited until the three had gone inside the barn, watching as they pushed Kay, who fell to her knees. They dragged her up and then pushed her through the door.

"Those fucking assholes. I will gladly poke the eyes out of every one of them," Sean said, enraged as he stood up.

Jack grabbed him and pulled him back down. "Keep yer voice doon, Sean. We knu. We knu. They assholes need tae pay fur murdering Katharine," Jack told him, conveying his concern about not being seen and his own anger at the violence these criminals had brought to their quiet homeland.

James brought the drone home, keeping it high in the sky until it was overhead. "C'moan, let's git oot o' 'ere. We kin goo straecht dae th' polis ward fum 'ere." James carefully packed his prized possession, his drone, back in its case, closed it, and they all headed back to the car.

~~~~~~~~~~

Finally, someone shows up at a reasonable hour, thought James. Three people got out of the white sedan with yellow and blue squares wrapping around it, clearly indicating the police. Inspector Chan, DCI Ferguson, and Detective Tanaka greeted James at the door. "Glad yer a' 'ere. Ah have th' video set up 'n' red e' ta' shaw ye," James told them.

One by one, they all shook his hand as they entered the house. Isa had just brought in a tray of Welsh rarebit still hot from the oven and sat it down on the table in front of the couch. She looked at the three and offered, "Kin ah git a'body a heavy?"

DCI Ferguson spoke, "Na ma'am, we ur oan duty. 'N' right noo we wantae keep oor best wits aboot us." May Ling and Akio nodded, agreeing with the DCI.

James set the video to play on the small television, the only one Isa allowed in the house. They all huddled close together to be in front of the screen as the video played.

As it ended, Sean asked, "We go tonight to rescue her, right?"

DCI Ferguson answered, "Furst, 'n' that is how come we ur 'ere, tae discuss options. Whit ah have is; one, we kin send in a wee gang o' Special Forces men; two, we kin surround th' building wi' oor SWAT teams 'n' hit thaim wi' a surprise assault; or three, we kin try a go tae contact Logan Shaw 'n' see if we kin arrange a trade o' some sort."

May Ling was shaking her head. "That ruthless bastard can't be trusted to make a deal. I vote we hit him hard with the SWAT team at the house. But we send in the Special Forces team to set up just outside the barn. When the fireworks start at the house, they move in to find Kay and secure the barn area."

A quick scan of the room saw Akio, Sean, Pistachio, James, Jack, and Isa all nodding. Sean stood up, turning toward DCI Ferguson. "That gets my vote. I mean, vote or not, I want it that way! I think May Ling is right. We cannot trust Shaw. This is by far the best plan for saving Kay. And as I look around, everyone agrees. Can you do it?"

DCI Ferguson had a sinister grin on his face. "Dae it? Laddie, ah have bin waiting years fur an opportunity tae git that scumbag Shaw. I'll have th' teams plan 'n' practice th'morra. Th'morra night we gang in. Ony objections?"

Getting in the Spirit

The morning light brought the sound of roosters crowing and work tending the sheep, chickens, and various other animals that made the MacDuff farm their home. Isa hoped chores would help keep Sean focused while they waited. Once finished, they sat around the table while Isa scurried about cooking and served them a traditional breakfast of square Lorne sausage, fried egg, baked beans, tattie scones, fried tomatoes and mushrooms, and toast.

"Sorry wee jimmies ah have na coffee, only Scottish tea. Bit tis git plenty o' caffeine if that's whit ye be wanting," Isa told them, as she set down a plate filled with more tattie scones hot out of the oven, wiping her hands on her apron.

"Isa, no more, please. It's not that I don't appreciate it, I do. It's just under the circumstances, I'm not hungry right now," Sean said solemnly.

Pistachio had just taken a large bite of sausage when his cell phone rang. Pulling it from his pocket, he did his best to chew and swallow.

"Haylo mada. Yah. Yah. Wi did discover Kay a alive an a shi is being held captive eena ah barn. Da police a goin' do ah raid tonite. Yah. Yah. Really? Yah mi will. Mi luv yuh tuh mada."

"Agwe?" Sean asked.

"Yah, mi mada. Mi not kno how shi do it. Buh mi kno shi duh. Shi areddi kno Kay is alive an ah prisoner. Shi a goin' perform har Voodoo rituals every nite until Kay a safe. Shi also ask if wi wud ask Bonnie, yuh frend Isa, you say is ah Druid Witch, tu do da same ting. An shi wants you an mi Sean, tu go da barn an place da three dolls shi gave us roun da barn eena ah triangle, lakka pyramid. As close as wi can," he nodded, "and shi say not tu git caught. Lakka wi a going tu try an git ourselves caught."

Isa smiled. "Ah awready love yer mither. 'N' ah if ah undurstan whit ye said, aye, ah wull ask Bonnie tah' apply her craft th' night as weel."

"You know, I truly appreciate everyone wanting to help in this. But, and I really don't want to hurt anyone's feelings, I don't buy into any of this mumbo jumbo magic stuff. Voodoo and witchcraft. I would really rather no one else, but the police are involved in this raid and rescue. They need to be able to concentrate on what they're doing without any kind of interference. You know?" Sean finished and then broke off a piece of tattie scone, plopping it resolutely into his mouth.

"Oh mon. Mi haffta tell you Sean. Mi undastan your reluctance tuh use mi madda or Bonnie. Buh let mi tell you mi have seen mi madda duh tings dat sen shivers up mi spine. Shi da real deal. Besides mon, eff you nu believe eena any ah dis mumbo jumbo den you should't haffta worry bout any interference as neither ah dem will evah be out of dem houses."

"He's right, Sean," Jack said. "You can't have it baith ways. If ye don't beleeve, then thay can't dae anythin' tae interfere. If ye dae beleeve, then trust me, thay kin hulp in ways th' polis can't even magine. Ah have seen Bonnie dae tings na human shuid be able tae dae."

"Wait! Wait, wait, crawling around in the dark anywhere near that place to stick three silly dolls is exactly what I call interfering. And it's dangerous. If they find a doll, they'll know someone's on to them."

"Nuh one will tink ah doll laying inna bushes means anyone is on tuh dem," Pistachio responded.

"Ye knu guys, mah drone juist happens tae have a

delivery attachment. It's a three-prong claw that opens, lik' putin money in thi slot ene one of tem contraptions whaur ye try tae grab th' stuffed animal. Ah push th' button whin a'm waantin' it tae open 'n' drap whitevur it's haulin'. Ah kin fly th' drone near th' barn 'n' drap thaim in th' lanky grass. 'N' as ah bought th' drone wi' th' deluxe package, ye wull be pleased tae knu it haes night vision," James boasted.

Sean listened as he chewed, then took a sip of tea thinking intensely. "Isa, holy cow, that is some strong tea. I'm already starting to sweat."

Isa nodded, "Aye, 'tis."

"James, I'll tell you what, if you can do that, and as you say, our two ladies in their kitchens stirring potions can hardly interfere, then okay, let them do it. I'm just scared. Scared shitless. I want my Kay back safe, in my arms. If Bonnie and Agwe can help, what the hell? Let's throw everything, including the whole damn kitchen sink at them."

"Aye, that's th' spirit!"

~~~~~~~~~~

The teams (Team One: Special Ops, composed of six men and one woman, and Team Two: SWAT, composed of ten men and two women) reviewed the video over and over until they formulated a plan.

Professionals at the highest level, they laid out mock floorplans of the house and barn close to the same size as their objective in the rear parking lot of the station. They spent the afternoon running the procedure repeatedly, working on timing and communications.

DCI Ferguson, Akio, and May Ling watched several of the enactments before heading back to Ferguson's office.

"Thay luk guid. It's a simple operation. Bit, they're a' seasoned enough tae knu it's th' easy ones that Murphy likes tae fuck with th' most. 'Tis tae late tae dae it this forenicht, we gang th'morra nicht. Th' waither looks best th'morra nicht as weel. Warm, na clouds, na smirr. It's a'maist a full moon so thay won't need tae be usin' thair headlamps unless absolutely necessary. It's mirk at seven-thirty, bit we ur aff tae hauld yer horses 'til eleven. Gie thaim time tae relax 'n' dram a heavy ar two tae slow thair response time. Th' flash grenades wull goin' aff oan th' side o' th' hoose furthest fom th' barn tae draw thair attention thare. That is whin team one wull move oan th' barn. Wance Shaw's men come ootdoors, thaan wull descend oan thaim, again trying tae push thaim awa' from th' barn. Everything looks guid, we juist need lassie luck tae be oan oor side th'morra night."

Even the Kitchen Sink

Sean was beside himself when May Ling called to tell him that the rescue wouldn't happen that evening. He was worried the gang might change plans and move, taking Kay with them or, worse, kill her right on the spot. But he also understood the need for everything to be as optimal as possible for their success. Once the raid started, there was no turning back. The only way Kay would come out alive was if these two teams were given their greatest advantage.

Pistachio took it as an opportunity. "Sean, mi kno how yuh feel bout wah mi mada can duh as ah Voodoo priestess. Buh, mi waan tuh point out eff wi hab dis evening tuh use shud'n we drive up there an si eff wi able tuh place di three Nkisi dolls. Wi mite even ketch ah glimpse ah Kay," he added to strengthen his suggestion.

Isa nodded. "Ah gree. Pistachio's muther kin well offer whit we need tae have th' advantage. A'm aff tae gang see Bonnie tae see howfur ah can—I mean howfur we kin hulp in her summoning th' spirits tae align wi' us th' night 'n' especially th'morra night."

James and Jack entered the living room at that moment. Seeing the concern on Sean's face and hearing the tail end of Isa's statement about Bonnie, the brothers knew well something was up for tonight.

"Whit kin ah dae?" Jack asked.

"Whit kin we dae, ye sheep's bahookie," he said giving his brother a lighthearted shove.

With Sean still quiet, digesting everything, Pistachio took the initiative to answer the twins.

"Wi need tuh drive up tonite tuh da same spot wi did

before tuh see if wi can, widout being seen, tek da three dolls mi madda did giv us an wants placed a roun da barn. Wi hab jus bin told da raid a on for tomorrow nite."

"Whit ur we sittin' aroond waiting fur? Let's dae it," James agreed.

"Wait, we have two hours 'til th' sun sets, bit ah think lik' lest time, let's dae this after midnight whin thay have hud few tae mony heavies. James, git yer drone charged up, I'll fill th' motor up wi' gas. Grab yer dolls," he laughed pointing at Pistachio. "That sounded a bit silly eh. Everyone whaur th' darkest clothing ye hae."

Sean nodded. "Okay. Everything, including the kitchen sink," he said, reminding himself of the need to use everything at their disposal.

Isa got up. "Guid then ah hae time tae mak' dinner fur a' o' ye. Ah pure wantae see those dolls Agwe made fur ye. Kin ye bring thaim intae th' scullery?"

Eena Har Element

Eerily dark, only candles lit Agwe's living room that overlooked the Caribbean Sea toward Cuba. There were lots of candles of various sizes and colors and a large ceramic bowl that was smoldering, impelling pungent, whitish blue smoke toward the low ceiling, filling the room with the scent of herbs. In the shadows of the room, occasionally lit by the flickering flames from the candles, were seven women, members of Agwe's group. They hummed quietly and chanted, to the beat from a lone man with long thick dreadlocks pounding out a steady rhythm on his conga. Agwe, barefooted, was dressed all in white except for the colorful scarf tied around her head to hold back her grey and black hair. Beads of perspiration glistened on her forehead as she danced around, stopping to draw lines on the floor for her Veve, a beacon to the loa. She knelt, carefully drawing on the concrete floor various artistic symbols using a powder from a smaller bowl. Yellow in color, it consisted of ground eggshell, corn meal, wood ash, and gunpowder.

After finishing each symbol, Agwe stood up and danced with total abandon to the beat of the conga. Spinning and chanting, she shook a colorfully painted gourd with a bone handle over the symbols and danced on them until they were obliterated. Then, using her hand, she brushed out a new area to draw more symbols.

Drinking rum straight from the bottles, as they were passed about, they continued the ritual until beams of morning sunlight pierced the blinds. They would rest and start again when the sun dipped once more into the ocean's horizon, creating the much sought-after green flash.

116

Bonnie Bòideach

Almost 5,000 miles away, participating harmoniously, connected only in spirit, was the Druid wise woman, Bonnie Bòideach. She needed no coaxing to aid her friend Isa and try to help protect those involved in their attempt to rescue Kay.

Isa had witnessed Bonnie's rituals of white witchcraft a few times, but never like this, never participating as she was this evening. As was Agwe, both lassies were barefooted to ground with Mother Earth. They wore naturally dyed, solid dark blue, hand-spun wool dresses and tartan earasaid scarves, fastened with a copper brooch, allowing the long scarves to cascade nearly to their feet. Both being widowed, their husbands having passed on years before, they wore their hair bound by a simple snood to signify their status, thereby carrying on hundreds of years of Celtic tradition.

Isa's large kitchen table, a scullery buird, had been carried and set up outside to be used as an altar in the center of the circle. It was adorned with many candles, charms, flowers, and herbs (pearlwort, St. John's wort, purple wild hyacinth, and juniper berries), all laid out with crystals in a unique pattern. In the middle of the table was a small cast iron cauldron, heated by a more contemporary means: a can of Sterno.

In the cauldron, Bonnie simmered spring water drawn from a natural well near the house and cuttings from the plants that adorned the table. As the herb's fragrance rose with the steam, Bonnie withdrew from her dress a small leather pouch and carefully removed several items, which she then dropped into the potion: a frog stone, some snail beads, and several copper coins. In front of the cauldron stood a poppet made from wax and corn husks wrapped in linen. The effigy, made earlier, had already been presented to the women of her coven, who passed it around while chanting, "This is Logan Shaw, this is Logan Shaw," channeling his dark spirit into the poppet.

Bonnie and Isa performed a slow dance around the altar three times. After stopping in front of the simmering, steaming cauldron, Bonnie walked to the northern point just beyond the altar. She raised a small lantern into the air to welcome each of the Guardians:

"We bid ye hail 'n' welcum guardians o' th' Watchtower o' th' North element o' Earth," and set down a bowl filled with salt, tossing some on the ground to represent soil. Using her staff, she scribed an arc in the dirt to the easternmost point and repeated:

"We bid ye hail 'n' welcum guardians o' th' Watchtower o' th' East element o' Earth." Isa brought her a ceramic incense burner that Bonnie lit to symbolize air. Continuing her inscribed line, she then walked to the southern point and again spoke holding the lantern high:

"We bid ye hail 'n' welcum guardians o' th' Watchtower o' th' South element o' Earth." Isa brought her a candle this time to represent fire. Once more, she scribed the arc until she reached the westernmost point:

"We bid ye hail 'n' welcum guardians o' th' Watchtower o' th' West element o' Earth." Isa brought her a bowl of water, which Bonnie sprinkled on the ground. Finally closing the arcs to form a circle, she spoke to the Watchtowers:

"Th' circle is open but unbroken. Let us begin."

Hour after hour, stopping only occasionally, they continued the slow dance around the table-turned altar. Each third dance around the table, Bonnie would repeat an Eolas, a rhyme or limerick, three times.

The two older lassies kept their ritual going throughout the evening until they heard from the twins. Then they retreated to the house to rest, knowing the following morning they would need to prepare everything all over again so as to repeat the ritual the night of the raid.

Not quite the debauchery of Agwe with her rum, Isa and Bonnie still managed to polish off a bottle of twelve-year-old single malt between them during their night of ritual.

"We might be getting a bit auld fur this kind o' behavior," Bonnie said, sitting down for a rest and smoke of her pipe.

"Na, Bonnie, wur juist getting guid at it," Isa replied, holding up her glass of golden liquid to Bonnie and to Guardians the Watchtowers.

Dropping In

Heading back to the same spot from which they originally launched the drone, Jack turned off the headlights as they got close, navigating by the glow of the nearly full moon. The only sounds were the engine and the tires rolling over the dirt and gravel road. Eager to get started, Jack opened the driver's door, which instantly set off a loud beeping noise as the keys were still in the ignition. He responded quickly, yanking the keys out, silencing the beep. They sat motionless, listening to see if there might be a response from below. Several minutes passed, then they quietly got out of the car, heading over to the rocks they had hidden behind before.

James set the box down and then held up his finger to his lips. "Shhh."

He took his time opening the box and setting up the drone. Once it was ready to fly, he asked Pistachio for a doll. Pistachio reached into his pack, pulling out the first of the hand-carved wooden dolls. James took it, turning it over in his hands to look at it before hooking it to the claw that would securely hold it. He looked at the other three men.

"'Ere we gang." Using the control pad, he sent the drone high into the night sky.

This time there were four heads side by side staring at the tiny screen. The night vision image was a yellowish-green and black, but the detail was remarkably clear. James navigated the drone to the northeast corner of the barn. As he lowered the drone closer to the ground, they could see a small creek with heavy brush on both sides.

"Perfect," he said quietly and released the claw's grip on the doll. They all watched as it bounced once and settled near the bushes.

"Nice, James," Sean told him.

James brought the drone home taking it high in the air first before returning. He looked at Pistachio and held up two fingers.

Pistachio pulled out the second doll, the most beautifully crafted of the three. It was the one Agwe made especially for Kay. Pistachio handed it to James.

"Da one belongs tuh Kay."

James repeated the process and, this time, flew over the barn to the west side. He lowered the drone, looking for a place with tall grass to drop it. The only tall grass was further away than the first drop by some thirty feet. He looked at Pistachio. "That's as claise as ah dare git

Pistachio nodded and looked to Sean for his reaction. Sean nodded back. Once again, the claw disengaged, and the doll hit the ground, bouncing several times before landing on its feet.

Jack lightly slapped James on the back. "Naat baad brother. Tae baad ye can't land yer darts that weel." Chiding him on his recent poor performance tossing darts where two ladies one night recently had them buying round after round at their favorite pub each time they lost a game. "Ah thought ah scored them perfectly," he said, smiling coyly at Jack.

The drone returned, and Pistachio handed James the third and last doll. He hooked the doll with the claw and flew it up and toward the barn, then over the barn toward the east side, when suddenly the doll fell free from the claws, hit the roof, and bounced down the roof's pitch and off, landing only a few feet from the building, in plain sight.

"Crap," James mumbled. "Ah kin grab it. Ah kin git it wi' th' claw. Whit dae ye think, shuid ah? Or shuid ah lea it whaur it is?" he asked, looking at Sean.

This was Sean's greatest fear, playing out in front of him on a tiny green and black screen. But one thing Sean was exceptional at was making tough decisions quickly. His mind briefly analyzed all of the options, even weighing in his own emotional response. He took a deep breath and asked, "How hard is it to grab something? I hope to hell not as difficult as those stupid vending machines."

Jack responded, "James is pure guid wi' that claw. Ah think he shuid gie it a shot."

"James?" Sean asked.

"If ah don't git it th' furst hav a go we'll stoap," James answered.

"Do it," Sean told him.

James navigated the drone over the doll, then, opening the claw all the way, started to lower it toward the ground. As it got close, dust started to kick up, making it impossible to see anything on the screen. James closed his eyes, and, counting silently, stopped the descent and closed the claw. Everyone held their breath as he slowly brought the drone back up into the air. As it rose out of the dust, the image became clear on the screen, and it was apparent that the doll was no longer lying in the open. James flew the drone over the tall grass he had originally intended to drop it, and, pressing the release button, they all watched as the third doll dropped to the ground.

Sean, breathing a huge sigh of relief, squeezed James' shoulder, "Well done. Bring it home, and let's get out of here."

Inside the barn, Kay and Elise were unable to sleep because of the pain from their injuries inflicted by the dogs and beatings at the hands of several of Shaw's men (not including

Bear). Bear had been one of the men who returned them to the barn, giving their wounds a final look over before following the other men back to the house.

Both women were conscious enough to be startled when they heard what sounded like a large cone or branch hitting the roof. They stared up, not saying a word. Then Kay heard what she was sure must be a fan. She pointed toward it without saying a word. Looking in the direction of the new noise, they both saw dust floating in through the cracks of the old barn wood, illuminated by the moonlight.

"What the hell was that?" Elise asked, moaning as she turned.

"I don't know. But I'm pretty sure it wasn't anything those assholes down at the house did. Not that it matters because we can't do anything about it," she said, holding up her chained wrists. "Let's just stay quiet and listen, see if we can hear anything else. Maybe by some miracle, there's someone walking around looking for us, and we can signal for help," Kay said with little conviction.

Guid Tae Go

Team One (Special Ops) and Team Two (SWAT) did their final briefing and equipment checks together. Then prepared themselves for the most grueling part of an operation like this: the wait. It was still early evening; dusk was passing to dark.

Communications was still going over a litany of items to be checked and double-checked, all with a crackle on the radio followed with a, "Guid tae go."

"The weather, is that still good?" DCI Ferguson asked.

"Aye, we shaw hee haw oan th' doppler. It wull be cuul this forenicht, bit clear," crackled ower th' tranny."

On the other side of the globe, it was still light. Agwe started preparations early in anticipation of the evening's events taking place in Scotland. Pistachio had called in the morning to give her the details of the impending raid and to let her know they had been successful in placing the dolls around the barn.

"Good, very good. Tonite wi plae," Agwe said, letting out a chilling and sinister laugh that Pistachio had never heard his mother express. A laugh that sent shivers up his shoulders, neck to the top of his scalp.

Knowing they were all exhausted from the previous evening and wanting to give them energy for the next round, Agwe prepared an unusual meal for her sleeping companions. Purposely making enough noise to rouse her followers, she made ackee and saltfish, fried dumplings, and Jamaican hot chocolate tea, bringing it all out on a large tray.

"Yuh goine ta' be needing dis. Wi hab lots ah rum tuh drinkz tonite," she said, and once again let out the sinister cackle-like laugh.

Tossing a handful of dried fruits and leaves into the ceramic bowl, she lit them. Once they started burning, she blew out the flames to let the smoke rise and permeate the house.

"Ah mi luv di smell ah fruit incense inna mawning," she said and let out the sinister laugh even louder.

As night fell on the MacDuff ranch, Bonnie and Isa made their final preparations as well. This time they included the twins, Sean and Pistachio. Bonnie brought more of her crystals, rocks, and candles, and Jack brought out a load of kindling and peat, enough to keep the fire in the pit near the circle glowing all night.

James and Jack both wore their kilts, complete with tartan shawl, belt and clan buckle, sporran, hose with flashes, and tall leather boots. Isa rummaged around in the attic to find and bring down two wool reddish-brown Celtic ritual robes with hoods and yokes that covered the shoulders, offering them to Sean and Pistachio.

"Ye lads look right official fur th' evenin," Bonnie told them, then asked. "Isa, dae ye still have yer lute?"

"Aye, it's even tuned. Ah was playing it a tae o' nights ago." She went to her room, returning with the lute, which she handed to Bonnie. Taking it from her, Bonnie strummed several simple chords and then motioned for Sean and Pistachio to join her as she sat down. "I'm gonna shaw ye a tae o' simple chords a'm waantin' ye tae tak' turns playing thought th' forenicht. If ye kin wi'oot stopping."

"I'll give it a go. But I've been trying to learn guitar since I was a kid, and all I know are few simple chords," Sean told her.

Pistachio was grinning. "Mi not supose you ave steel drum anyweh?"

"Na laddie, it's th' lute or ye whistle," Bonnie joked.

Pistachio pursed his lips and blew a shrill whistle.

"Maybe mi bess stick wid da lute. Ah couple ah chords? Even an island boy lakka mi can learn dat. Show us, Bonnie," Pistahcio answered.

"Pray tae th' spirits o' th' universe. James, dae ye still have yer tabor drum?"

"Ah dae, Bonnie. Jack is guid oan th' lute. Pistachio, ye lik' drums, ye kin hulp me. Ye 'n' ah kin tak' turns keeping a steady beat. Tis na steel drum mynd ye. We'll be a regular rock 'n roll band," James replied, with a snicker.

"Haw, lik' ye cuid ever haud a beat or a note," Jack joked back.

"Wee jimmies, ah don't need tae point oot th' serious nature o' this forenicht, dae ah?" Isa scolded.

With A Little Help From Our Friends

Kay woke with every muscle in her body throbbing in pain from the dog bites, which were now swollen and most likely infected. The punishment beating that she and Elise had received, and being shackled hand and foot to a post, didn't help. She did her best to stretch, moving one muscle group at a time, relying on what she had learned in the yoga class she had started in college. Glancing over at Elise, she gasped, alarmed as it didn't appear she was breathing. "Elise!" she said, loud enough for Elise to hear, but she hoped, not enough to alert the men down in the house. Elise coughed, moving as she did. In an odd way, witnessing her suffering comforted Kay. It meant Elise was alive.

It was dark. Kay could see stars through the cracks of the barn's old wood siding. She didn't know what time it was, but it was early enough in the evening that the full moon wasn't yet up. She stared through the boards lamenting their predicament. As far as she knew, there had been no further noises. No one was outside looking for them. She knew Sean would be working with the police, but she also knew he didn't have a clue where to look. *We're so screwed!* she thought, allowing the negative truth to surface.

As the thought passed over her synapses, staring through the cracks, the star she had been looking at disappeared. Then another. *There's a storm coming in*, she thought, not knowing whether that was a good or bad omen. It didn't really matter. They weren't getting out of the barn without help. A lot of help.

A new noise caught her attention. She strained to listen. It was raindrops on the barn's roof. The rain was short-lived, stopping

127

as quickly as it started. She laid back against the post to which she was chained, feeling the weight of her body in ways she never had before.

When she awoke again, the smell of dampness and air charged with negative ions permeated the inside of the barn. She could tell the full moon was up now as its light streamed through the boards. It was oddly pleasant, considering the circumstances. She watched as the fog rolled in between the boards.

So pretty, she thought. *Wow, didn't think it was going to storm tonight. What next, thunder and lightning?*

Suddenly there was a brilliant flash, followed almost immediately by a loud, explosive cracking sound that dissipated into the distance, echoing off the surrounding hills. It made both Kay and Elise sit straight up against their posts. They looked at each other as fog now poured in through the cracks.

"That scared the shit out of me. I was dreaming those assholes were going to shoot me," Elise said in an alarmed voice.

"We're okay. It's just a thunderstorm. Which is good, maybe it will keep those jerks down in the house, so they won't want to bother with us tonight," Kay offered.

Again, the interior of the barn was lit up by a flash just outside, followed by an immediate boom that crackled off into the distance. Echoing off the rocky hills behind the barn that Kay had seen as she was being dragged back to the barn. They were alone in this world and had no idea where they were.

"Shit, that was close. I mean really close," expressed Kay, listening for any other sounds while she did her best to survey the inside of the barn. But the moonlight was now hidden by fog.

128

"The fog here is pretty intense. I thought it got thick in San Francisco. This stuff you can hold in your hand." Elise laughed, then coughed and held her chest, but she had smiled, and that relieved Kay greatly.

Kay was returning the smile across their divide, but thinking to herself, *Shit she's getting pneumonia*. Then a dark shadowy figure ran between them, fog trailing off it, and then disappeared, running straight through the side of the barn. Kay screamed, bringing her chained hands to her mouth.

"What the hell was that?" she squealed.

Elise sat wide-eyed and paralyzed by fear. In a trembling voice, she said, "It looked like a cat. A big cat. You know, like a bobcat or mountain lion. Except, Kay, I could see through it."

Kay nodded. "I know. What the hell is going on?"

This time the flash and boom were simultaneous, bathing the entire barn interior in bright, almost blinding light. It spooked Kay so badly that she hit her head on the post. As she did, in the flash, she saw something against the wall closest to her. She tried to focus on it as another flash and boom rattled the building. Still staring in the direction of the object, she saw it fall out of the shadows toward her, landing only a few feet away. She stared in disbelief. There, laying but a few feet from her, where moments before it was hidden in the barn's dark shadows against the aging wood walls, were a pair of rusted bolt cutters.

The first thought that went through her mind was, *maybe Bear, who never really hurt us, left them there for us so we could escape*. Then she thought, *no, there is just something really strange going on here*. She closed her eyes to think. When she opened them, she saw a larger-than-life image of the hand-carved Nkisi doll Agwe had given her, as if made from the fog itself, floating above the bolt cutters. It was trying to say something or chant, but there was no sound. Then another flash and boom, and the apparition was gone.

"Did you see that?" Kay exclaimed excitedly.

Elise could only nod.

"Look over there," Kay said, pointing to the bolt cutters. "The Voodoo doll was showing it to me."

"Voodoo? What Voodoo?" Elise asked, straining to see what she was pointing at.

"Before we left Jamaica, Pistachio's mother–oh wait–you don't know that part of the story. Sean and I fled San Francisco to Jamaica, trying to get away from the two Japanese men you met. Well, they followed us there, and you will be very pleased to know they are both dead and at the bottom of the ocean. Another story for another day, and girl, there's going to be another day." Kay turned to see Elise smile. "See, we went to visit Sean's relative in Jamaica. Her name is Agwe Morrison, and she is a real live, honest-to-God Voodoo priestess. Her son's name is Pistachio. Let me tell you; he is a coin with more than two sides. But he saved our lives there, putting his own life in danger. So, he came with us. You'll like him.   What I am trying to say is, Agwe made three dolls. Voodoo Nkisi dolls. They were supposed to protect us. I thought it was nice but silly. No, I thought it was stupid. I don't believe in that kind of hocus pocua, or any kind of supernatural magic. But, Elise, that was a supersized version of the same doll she gave me. I mean, what the fuck? And those—those right there—are bolt cutters. If I can reach them, girl, we won't need the circular knitting needles those shitheads took from me. We'll be outta here. Do you think you can run?"

With home in her eyes, Elise said, "Kay, darling, this

time I will fly!"

~~~~~~~~~~

Logan Shaw was looking out the living room window at the deck.

"Whaur th' hell did this faug come fae? Ah read this efternoon 'twos supposed tae be clear a' week." As he finished, a bright blue and white streak from the heavens lit up the deck, followed by a thunderous boom. It was loud and made him step back. Stumbling, he braced himself with a hand on the bar so as not to fall, but still managed to spill his drink all over himself.

Several of the men laughed, to which he responded, "Mibbie ye wid lik' me tae skelp ye round a bit?"

"C'moan boss, ye knu we ur only funnin' ye. This faug 'n' lightening git us a' crept oot. Let me pour ye anither gless a whisky," Bear offered.

"Aye, aye. I'll git me oan. Why come don't th' lot o' ye goin' up 'n' check oan our bargaining chips in th' barn?" Logan said, reaching for the good Scotch, the real Scotch, to refill his glass. As he did, there was another flash and simultaneous boom that shook the house and caused him to pour his drink all over himself yet again.

"Hell's bells. Goin' oan, ga check on th' girls," he shouted. "Shit, a'm needin' tae chaynge. Don't let me be hearing ony snickers, I'll smack yer ears."

Three of the men pulled on their coats, grabbed

flashlights, and tried their best to get the two Dobermans to follow them. It was not to be. Both well-trained animals were having no part in being outside in the flashes of thunderous lightning.

"Bloody wimps," Bear teased, though not at all eager himself to head out of the house and take the little path that led up to the barn. As the three stepped outside and closed the front door, the fog seemed to increase. They could barely see the end of the deck.

Knowing the way by heart, Bear led the way. He wanted to check on the girls first in hopes of convincing the other two that the captives were secure. He hoped he could convince them to return to the house before they were tempted to take advantage of their prisoners. He was counting on his fellow louts not wanting to be out in this cold and fog any longer than they had to.

He had traveled but a few feet from the house when a phantom appeared on the deck behind him but in front of his companions. The phantom composed itself from the swirling fog until it was clearly a snorting and snarling boar with huge glistening tusks. Not seeing the apparition, Bear continued toward the barn.

The other two men, Boyd and Murdoch, backed up to the door only to find it locked. They pounded on it, but with no one responding quickly, they both ran off the front side of the deck toward the cars. Off the deck, the fog was so thick that they had to put their hands in front of them to feel where they were going. Another brilliant blue and white bolt struck the ground in front of them, knocking them both to the ground. The flash was so bright that they momentarily, while on their hands and knees, could see the van, but they could also see another specter forming in the grey mist. A death adder, three or four times its normal size, swirled out of the fog between the two men, hissing and whipping its forked tongue back and forth.

The snake appeared to be rising into the air, rising up at least five feet from its coiled tail. Boyd, closest to the deck and scared beyond rational thought, drew his pistol from his belt and shot at the hallucination. The snake instantly disappeared, and he heard a thud of something hitting the ground. Petrified, he crawled to where his partner, Murdoch, lay sprawled out, grabbing his throat with blood gushing out between his fingers. Boyd looked in horror, knowing it was he that had accidentally shot him.

"I'm sorry. In th' name o' God, a'm sae sorry," he cried as the man closed his eyes and stopped moving.

Hearing the shot, a half-dressed Logan Shaw ran downstairs and out onto the deck with a rifle in his hands, only to find he couldn't see a thing because of the fog. He stood perfectly still, listening for any noises.

Suddenly, in front of him, a spirit appeared out of the fog in the form of a monstrous snarling and snapping wolf. The wolf growled, a horrendous guttural sound while exposing its translucent saber-like teeth. Staring directly at Logan, with its glowing red eyes penetrating the fog, the monster dropped to its haunches, huge muscles twitching as it prepared to spring on its prey, fog rising off of the apparition like smoke.

Thare ur na wolves anymair, they're extinct popped into his mind, then without so much as trying to aim his rifle, with the gun at his hip, he pulled the trigger and ducked.

Hearing the first shot, Bear assumed the police had arrived and decided his best option was to make a run for the Highland, only to feel a burning sensation in his right leg followed by the crack of a rifle being fired. He dropped to the ground and held his leg, doing his best to be still and quiet.

Hearing the second gun go off, Boyd stood up to try to get in the van. As his hand wrapped around the sliding door handle, a bolt of lightning struck the van, sending a charge of electricity through his body that threw him ten feet back toward the deck. He lay there smoldering, trying to understand what had just happened as he slipped into the darkness of death.

Logan froze, horrified by the bolt of lightning that lit the macabre scene and forced him to watch as Boyd was hurtled toward himself and the deck. It was rare for this lifelong criminal, who had seen his share of death, to ever be scared, but right then, he was terrified.

~~~~~~~~~~

Kay did her best to rotate her body toward where she had seen the bolt cutters fall into the hay covering the floor. To her advantage, the floor was starting to become illuminated by the moon's rays. The clouds had cleared over the barn, allowing the moon to shine. One beam, shining through the boards, landed on the head of the bolt cutters. Kay looked dismally at the cutters, for she could clearly see they were at least a foot away from her outstretched arm. It might as well have been a mile. She looked around to see if there was a stick or tool she could use to bridge the distance. Nothing.

Seeing her problem, Elise knew a piece of chain they did not use to bind her lay right next to her. She grabbed and waved it at Kay, trying to get her attention, but finally just threw it toward Kay. Her toss was close enough that it landed on Kay's leg, making her scream. Turning, she saw what it was, and Elise smiling and pointing.

"Well done, girl. Hold on one sec," Kay said, mustering up what little strength she had left to sit up and grab the chain off her leg. Then, laying down and wiggling as far as she could, she grabbed one end of the chain firmly and tossed the other end toward the bolt cutters. It landed right on target between the handles, but when she pulled on the chain, it slipped over and off. Not to be denied, she tried again and again until, finally, one of the links lodged itself between where the handles came together. She pulled until it was snug, then slowly pulled the cutters inch by inch toward her until she could reach them.

Overjoyed at her accomplishment, she tried to open the cutters. They were old and rusty and didn't want to budge. Kay stopped to breathe, to relax.

"You can do this, Wonder Woman," Elise threw out to embolden her.

"Yes, I can, damn it." With that and a great deal of grunting, she pried the two handles apart to open the bolt cutters. "Whew." Taking another quick breather, she then tried to move them into position to cut the links on her right leg. As she got the jaws onto the link, there was a gunshot. She stopped. Looking at Elise, she asked, "Oh shit. What now?"

"Well, don't wait to find out; cut that thing off of you!" Elise yelled at her.

Kay didn't require any further coaxing. She grabbed both handles and, with all of her might, pulled them together until she heard the wonderfully satisfying crisp "snap" sound of the link breaking in two.

"Oh my God. It worked."

None of the links were easy to break, especially in-between lightning strikes and another gunshot. But, finally, Kay and Elise could move about unrestrained. They both still wore metal cuffs on their arms and legs but were no longer bound to the posts. They were free.

Elise held her arms up and wiggled her wrists. "They're the latest thing, darling. Got them at Macy's." They both laughed and hugged.

"Love you, girl. I truly love you," Kay said. "Now come on. We need to put some distance between us and this old barn."

They managed to squeeze out through the same place as their last escape attempt, but this time, instead of heading for the road, they followed the sole moonbeam that lit the way up the mountain into the Highlands.

They made it to the edge of some tall grass, some thirty feet away from the barn, when Kay tripped on something. She looked down to see her Nkisi doll. She gasped, then bent down and picked it up. "No one is going to believe me. No one," she told Elise as they disappeared into the Highland night, Kay tightly holding on to the doll.

~~~~~~~~~~

Logan retreated to the front door he had left open. Inside, he told the only two gang members left to grab their guns. He pulled a jacket on over his cold shirtless body and then grabbed a briefcase lying on the table. "Let's git th' hell oot o' 'ere."

Through the fog, they made their way to the car in front of the van. All three stared at Boyd, lying in the dirt, still smoldering, then one by one, they stepped over him, and then walked around the lifeless body of Murdoch, still clutching his throat.

"Whit aboot thaim girls?" one of the men asked.

"Lea em. Get en th' ca an heid fur th' coast. Fur mah yacht," Logan said, crawling in the back and holding tightly to his briefcase and rifle.

They were several miles down the road, almost to town, when they passed a convoy of police vehicles headed to the house.

"Juist keep gaun. Smile 'n' keep gaun," Logan told the driver.

As Team One headed up above the barn, Team Two held back from the house out of sight. There was a small remnant of fog still floating low near the ground that was rapidly dissipating. The team leader for the Special Ops hopped out to look around, noting the ground was damp.

"How odd tae have faug tonight—ah bit that explains th' foosty ground," he said, looking at his sergeant, who was next out of the armored troop carrier. "Okay, everybody tak' yer positions," he ordered.

With the moon once again shining brightly, only a few clouds overhead, the men, as hoped, didn't require their night vision. They carefully advanced to within fifteen feet of the barn. The leader held up his fist, signaling the team to stop and wait for the flash grenades.

Below, Team Two drove up closer and then exited their vehicle, moving into their positions as practiced. The Team Two leader gave the signal, and two flash grenades swooshed into the air, landing on the far side of the deck. Suddenly, there was a blinding light and an incredibly loud explosion, followed by another only a few feet away. Two officers ran toward the front of the house, slowing to step over the two bodies before jumping onto the deck and then breaking the front door down. They rushed inside with rifles ready.

Hearing the grenades go off, Team One charged toward the barn, smashing through the old barn door. Inside, out of the moon's glow, they switched to night vision and started searching. Over and over, the leader heard, "Clear." When they had searched every corner and hay bale, they regrouped in the center.

"Leader two, leader one. We git an empty barn up 'ere. Bit, thare wur two fowk bein' held captive 'ere. Thair chain restraints have bin cut. Shaw's thugs mist have cut thaim tae lea in a hurry."

As with the barn, Team Two searched the house only to find it empty. They gathered on the deck to report.

"I din't know what happened here, sir, but we have two dee bodies outside, one shot, and one electrocuted." As he spoke, they all heard a moaning "Help" from the darkness near the barn. Two officers approached, rifles ready, to find Bear lying in the dirt, holding his leg, doing his best to quell the bleeding. He held one hand up to surrender, and the other he kept on his wound.

"Sur, we git one doon up 'ere, bit alive," the sergeant yelled. "He is guun tae need tae git tae th' hospital."

"Whit th' hell's bells guun oan 'ere if it wasn't us? A rival gang? What?" DCI Ferguson said, as he approached the carnage of the now-cleared area.

"Na hostages, 'n' na Logan Shaw. Mah bet is they're heading fur th' coast. Kin we git a chopper up th' night? Let's pat up some roadblocks—noow. They're oot thare, 'n' they're running," DCI Ferguson told dispatch over the radio.

Didn't Go As Planned

May Ling knocked on the door and waited. James answered and knew from looking at her that things had not gone as planned.

"Come in, inspector. We ur a' sittin' doon juist waiting tae hear fae ye or DCI Ferguson."

May Ling walked in to have all eyes turn toward her. Isa, who, being a hostess, was in her blood, got up and asked, "Kin ah git ye a heavy or a whisky inspector?"

Sean felt icy fear cascade through his body. With a deep sigh, he looked up at May Ling. "What—"

Before he could get the words out, May Ling answered what she knew he was going to ask. "She wasn't there. She either escaped, or they took her with them. But officers discovered two odd things. One, there was another hostage there with her. And two, the reason we think they might have escaped is that they were chained to a post, but the chains had been cut with a bolt cutter. If Shaw's men took them, they most certainly would have used a key on the locks."

Sean breathed a sigh of relief, hearing she hadn't been found dead. There was still hope.

"What about Shaw and his men?"

"Well, that's even more of a mystery. When our guys arrived, Kay wasn't there, and neither was Logan Shaw. But three of his men were. One was shot dead, another was electrocuted and was also dead, and the third was shot but is alive. He's in custody in the hospital. And no, he won't talk, and we don't have a clue what transpired on the scene before we got there. They have roadblocks set up and a helicopter in the air looking for them."

She stopped and, looking at Isa, said, "Yes, Isa, I would love a shot of whisky. Even better, make it a double."

"Nuh, mystery. Mada's Voodoo at plae," Pistachio offered.

"Aye 'n' Bonnie's Druid magic," added James, giving a nod and a smile to Bonnie.

"Well, it's a better answer than anything we have," May Ling responded, taking a long draw of the whisky Isa handed her, giving a little shiver at the end.

"Who's looking for Kay and whomever it is she might have escaped with?" Sean asked, feeling slightly more optimistic.

"Yes, well, we have Search and Rescue out now, combing the area. All we can do for the moment is wait," she said, throwing her head back and downing the last of her drink. "That Scotch is good stuff. Can I have another?" she asked.

As Isa got up to refill May Ling's glass, Bonnie excused herself having one last thing to do. Heading back out to the circle and the table, she picked up the poppet and, holding it high in the air, she then plunged the doll into the water in the cast iron cauldron and spoke to the Storm Kelpies, the Blue Men of Minch, beseeching them to intervene should Logan Shaw attempt to flee the island. She repeated two lines of a poem three times, then the final two lines she spoke but once. Leaving the doll submerged in the water, she retraced, in reverse, her steps opening the circle to close it. She returned inside, dusting her hands off as she did so, and sporting a bit of a confident smirk.

~~~~~~~~~~

"I just spoke with DCI Ferguson. He said Scottish Mountain Rescue has four of its ground teams working with two of the SARDA teams. That's at least 100 to 150 professionals who know the area better than those who live there. Plus, they have a helicopter and three SAUs in the air. He said they're searching from the barn and house in every direction," May Ling told Sean.

Sean nodded, sitting there feeling helpless.
"What's a SARDA team? And what's an SAU?" Sean asked, looking to participate by at least understanding what was going on.

"A good question and truly too long to say every time. SARDA stands for Search and Rescue Dog Association. An SUA is really just a drone. They call them 'small unmanned aircraft.' There are two police helicopters searching for Shaw and his gang. Ferguson said they've also assembled the largest contingent of police from Glasgow and Edinburgh, as well as all of the villages in between that he's ever seen. They're searching all the way to the coast," she answered, looking at a forlorn Sean. "We are going to find her, Sean."

He nodded and tried to smile, even though he knew, chances were, she was most likely already dead and in the trunk of Shaw's car. Pistachio recognized the hopelessness on Sean's face and came over to sit next to him.

"Yuh cannot let your mind tuh mek tings up based on tings wi don't kno. Wi do kno shi escaped, an wi do kno shi neva found, which can only mean shi a out deh alive an hiding," Pistachio said, choosing his words carefully so as not to say that no body was found.

"He is absolutely correct. Do not allow your imagination to control your thinking," May Ling said, backing up Pistachio's advice.

142

DCI Ferguson sat in his vehicle at a checkpoint just west of Barrhead. Listening to the radio traffic as he waited impatiently for some good news, his radio crackled.

"Polis one err. We have spotted th' motor. It's abandoned at th' marina in Greenock. Bobies ur arriving oan scene noo," the pilot of the Huey radioed.

Ferguson leaned forward, instinctively starting the engine of his yellow and blue police vehicle upon hearing the pilot.

"Let's git polis two ower thare 'n' look for boats leavin' th' marina. Dispatch, send some men 'n' a detective ower tae th' marina. Let's see if Shaw owns a boat moored thare. Let me kno whit thay fin' in th' motor. A'm oan mah wey." His foot was already pressing hard on the pedal as he turned the car around, spraying gravel off the shoulder to head toward Greenock.

Guardians of the Watchtower

The full moon flooded the Highlands with soft light. Kay and Elise huddled together, doing their best to stay warm. Scared, in extreme pain, hungry, and thirsty, they managed to travel several miles uphill and toward what they thought might be the lights of Barrhead off in the distance.

The clear skies allowed a trillion stars to shine above them and made it much cooler than normal. Kay was in jeans and a T-shirt, while Elise was still wearing the light cotton summer dress that she had worn at the fair in Marin. It was truly a testament to their will to survive for both to have made it so far on bare feet that were cracked and bleeding but mercifully numb. They heard no sounds except the occasional, reassuring humming noise of crickets.

Kay, knowing they needed to rest and that she was not going to be able to remain conscious for much longer, grabbed a large stick and started digging out a bed of sorts in the rocky soil. She then pulled out, by the roots, handfuls of the tall grass to use as padding and cover for her and Elise. As she lay down next to Elise, she tossed more of the grass over them until they were covered.

"It's not much, and I hope this will keep us a tad warmer and camouflaged in case anyone makes it up this far looking for us. But, somehow, Elise, I think because of the gunfire, that they're long gone. Still, I'm not taking any chances." Kay snuggled in close to Elise to share their body heat. "Are you okay?"

Elise nodded and moaned but managed to get out a very optimistic, "Just peachy."

Kay started humming an old Chinese children's song

that her mom had hummed to her when putting her to bed at night. She was just drifting off when she saw yet another foggy apparition circling around where they lay. Trying her best not to move and draw attention to her and Elise, she slowly lifted her head up to watch. The misty phantom appeared to be a big grey wolf that she could see right through.

Remembering her talk earlier with Jack about predators that might attack his flock of sheep, and specifically about wolves, she recalled him saying that they're extinct in Scotland. She thought to herself, *so, what the hell is that then?* She felt no fear, as it wasn't coming any closer. The large animal just kept circling until another, and then another joined it. The three slowly circled until a fourth, much larger apparition joined them. Then one by one, they laid down at four separate points surrounding the girls.

Laying in the tall grass, their foggy appearance was more like smoke rising from the ground. Still, Kay could make out each figure well enough to detect differences in their appearance, color, size, and even demeanor. All four seemed to be guarding the women like a mother would watch over her children. Watching the ghostly visions lay down near her and Elise, she was overcome with a warm feeling of security. Unable to keep her eyes open any longer, Kay finally succumbed to exhaustion and fell into a deep sleep.

~~~~~~~~~~

Ferguson sat at his desk as May Ling and Akio came in.

"You have news, I believe?" May Ling asked, not sitting down.

Ferguson stood up, walking around his desk toward the dry eraser board he had set up with photos tapped to it, names written underneath, and black and red lines crisscrossing the various elements that somehow, in his mind, tied all the pieces together. He pointed to a photo from the Distillery with a body bag lying on the floor.

"We knu wha she is, th' lassie at th' distillery. Her DNA cam back 'n' we git a hit oan Interpol. Her name wis Kathy Mcquire. She was na angel. She didnae deserver tae be murdered, bit let's juist say her file is full. We ur bonny sure she was th' girlfriend o' a guy named Murdoch, wha is, sorry, wis one o' Logan Shaw's henchmen. He was fund deid at th' raid, shot in th' throat."

May Ling breathed a sigh of relief at the confirmation that it wasn't Kay.

"Any news on the car you found at the Marina?" she asked.

Ferguson turned to face her, still holding a dry eraser marker he was using as a pointer. "Aye. We knu thare wur three mibbie four fowk in th' motor. One was maist definitely Shaw." Ferguson chuckled. "In his hurry tae abandon th' motor, his wallet fell oot."

"No sign of Kay?" Akio asked before May Ling could.

Ferguson's face scrunched up into a grimacing frown.

"Weel, thare was na one else in th' motor, bit someone else hud bin in th' trunk. Thare was a substantial amount o' blood. It's oot fur testin right noo."

May Ling's head drooped. But undaunted, she asked, "Did Shaw have a boat moored at the Marina?"

Ferguson's frown changed to a slight smile, still a

grimace.

"Aye, that is some guid neews. He did, 'n' it's nae juist a boat it's a lairge yacht. That shouldn't be tae pernicketie tae spot. Th' RAF haes planes 'n' choppers searching th' area."

An older woman in a white lab coat knocked on the side of the open door.
"Excuse me, Danny?"

"Aye, whit did ye fin' oot, Deirdre?"

"Whoever th' jimmy was that was in th' trunk, is maist likely aye alive. Thare wisnae enough blood tae cause death."

May Ling looked up at the much taller lady to ask, "A man?"

"Aye, th' blood was frum a male," Deirdre said, reassuring May Ling and Akio.

"You said you thought there was another hostage in the barn. Could that be this guy in the trunk?" May Ling asked. She was already adding "a person X" to her own mental dry eraser board.

Ferguson turned back to his board, writing some notes under the photo of the abandoned car. "Indeed, cuid be."

~~~~~~~~~~

Kay had vivid dreams about giant grey wolves circling her all night. They chanted as they danced around her and Elise. Then the largest wolf walked up close to her and whispered in her ear. "We are the Guardians of the Watchtower and will protect you, will protect you, will protect

147

you..." She kept hearing the words repeated over and over as the wolf licked her face.

She reached up to touch the wolf in her dream but was instantly returned to painful consciousness. She felt the real fur of an animal licking her. Startled, she opened her eyes and saw an enormous gray wolf hovering over her. She panicked and tried to sit up and push the animal away as she heard a woman's voice loudly commanding, "Dagda, return!"

Kay looked toward the sound of the voice and saw a middle-aged woman with blondish red hair, wearing an orange vest walking toward her.

"Dagda, return!" she commanded again, pointing to the ground next to her. Dagda, a mostly gray German Shepherd, complied, returning to the woman in the vest and sitting down next to her. The woman was quick to give him a treat from a pouch on her belt. She brought a small walkie-talkie up to her mouth and, keying the device, said, "I've git thaim. Two lassies, alive."

She knelt down by Kay and pointed to her bright blue hair. "Kaylee Wu?" she asked, giving her a reassuring smile.

Kay started crying.

"Yes. I'm Kay, and this is Elise. Elise, wake up. Wake up!" she said, nudging Elise's back and forth, the chains from her wrists slapping her butt. "I was dreaming. Are you with the Guardians?"

"Na, Kay. They ca' me Elora 'n' I'm a member o' th' Scots Mountain Rescue gang, SARDA. This is Dagda, mah baby. Mah vert old baby, bit aye th' best search dug in bonnie Scotland. Urr ye 'n' yer mukker okay?" she asked.

"In my dream, I was surrounded by four giant wolves, and one kept saying, 'We are the Guardians of the Watchtower, and we will protect you, we will protect you.' That's when I woke up and saw your beautiful Dagda. Elise, wake up." She said again, pushing her harder.

Elise finally started moving and groaning. "I'm not doing very good, Kay," she said and started coughing.

Elora spoke into her walkie-talkie. "A'm needin' medical assistance up 'ere. Elise, kin ye tell me whit's wrong? Whaur tae ye hurt?"

"Everywhere," she said with a chuckle and then started coughing again.

May Ling picked up her cell phone. "Inspector Chan. Oh God, thank you. Who? No, say that again. That can't be. How in the hell did she get all the way over here? Okay, I'll meet you at the hospital." May Ling looked over at Sean. "Kay is okay. They just found her up in the Highlands. They're taking her to the hospital now for a check-up. But that's not the biggest news. I mean, I know for you, nothing could be more important, but the other hostage, the girl they just found with her," she paused, "is Elise Macdonald, Katharine Macdonald's granddaughter."

Sean stood up, his lips were moving, but he was unable to formulate any words.

"Want to ride in with Detective Akio and me?" she asked before he could say anything.

~~~~~~~~~~

It took them considerably longer than it should have to

reach the hospital. May Ling, driving a rental car, while trying to use her iPhone's GPS for directions, took them on an extended tour down several old dirt roads, twice driving into a ditch. Finally, with Sean navigating using Google Maps, they were able to pull into Royal Alexandra Hospital's parking lot. As they got out, she joked, "I'm a better inspector than I am a driver." Akio laughed.

DCI Ferguson was looking impatiently at his watch, worried about their drive taking so long. He immediately took them directly to the rooms where Kay and Elise were being examined. Sean, who not thirty-six hours ago thought the love of his life was deceased, found himself excited beyond anything he had ever experienced. They rounded the corner and came to two doors, each with an officer standing in front. A quick, mandatory flash of his badge and the officer stepped aside for DCI Ferguson. Inside, Kay was sitting up, talking to a nurse and a doctor. She lit up and screamed Sean's name when she saw him rushing toward her bed.

Not listening to the doctor or nurse, they hugged, rocking back and forth for several minutes before coming up for air. Kay then introduced the doctor and the nurse, who were both smiling at what they had just witnessed.

"Not a thing wrong wi' this young lassie that ye didn't juist fix wi' that hug. Some bites 'n' cuts we wull gie her antibiotics fur; ither than that, she kin lea wi`in th' hour," the doctor said, still wearing a satisfying grin from watching the reunion.

"Oh my God, Sean, Elise is here too. She's pretty beat up, but she'll be fine. That is one tough girl. She was already in the barn when they threw me in there," Kay said, still beaming.

May Ling put her hands on the bed rails.

"Kay, when they told me they found you and you were

150

okay, I was over the moon happy. Then they told me they had Elise, too. I made the officer repeat it several times to ensure I was hearing him correctly. When you can—no, as soon as you can—DCI Ferguson, Akio, and I need to talk to you about Logan Shaw. He and some of his men managed to escape. We believe they're on a yacht heading for Ireland. Did you see what happened? Two of his men are dead—one was shot, the other electrocuted. A third man was shot, but he'll survive. He's not talking much—yet."

"I'm ready to talk now. I'll do anything to help you catch those bastards. However, you might want to give Elise some time. She went through so much more than I did. She knows her grandma died. She knew before I told her. I told her the two Japanese men who murdered her were dead—" she paused, almost saying more than she knew she should. But it was enough to catch May Ling and Akio's attention. "—that is, that we heard they were killed by some fishermen in Jamaica."

Elise wanted out, and it showed; she was released the next day. DCI Ferguson picked her up and drove her out to the MacDuff ranch, where Isa had set up a small celebration. Sean, Pistachio, Kay, James, Jack, May Ling, and Akio were all there awaiting their arrival.

After everyone hugged Elise and was seated, eating and drinking, the two girls each relived what they had gone through, including how Elise managed to find herself in Scotland; the night of their first, failed, attempted escape, and the second attempt where they successfully got away in the fog, and the lightning. Kay wasn't sure she should but told them anyway about the foggy apparitions and the wolves that slept near them, guarding them.

Then James and Jack recounted how they used the

drone to find the barn and later placed the Nkisi dolls around the three points, as Agwe requested.

"Ah a'maist blotched it bad, dropping th' third doll. It landed oan th' barn roof 'n' rolled doon, falling in fron o' th' barn door. Whit a dumb bahookie, eh?"

"Aye, he's a bit of an uncoordinated bahookie fur a MacDuff, bit we loue him anyway," Jack teased.

"Whatever. He did some pretty fancy flying in my book, retrieving the doll, and then dropping it where it belonged," Sean said.

"That was what we heard," Kay said, looking at Elise. "We actually thought, hoped, it was someone looking for us. We knew it wasn't Shaw and his men. They had no reason to be throwing things up on the roof. But then the noise disappeared and with it, our hopes. Things were looking pretty bleak at that moment. We love you guys, you know that?"

Elise nodded, smiling.

Sean and Pistachio took turns trying to explain the simultaneous rituals that Agwe, Isa, and her close friend, the Druid witch Bonnie, had performed. Everyone sat spellbound, listening to each other's stories.

DCI Ferguson stood up, raising his glass in a toast. After reminding them it was dogged police work, Search and Rescue, and good luck that helped them, he then went on to offer a quick update.

"Ah don't wantae spoil this celebration talking aw the info aboot this nightmare, bit juist let me catch ye a' up on whaur th' investigation is. We don't knu whaur Logan Shaw is. Nor ony o' his gang that escaped wi' him. We ur still looking in open seas fur his yacht 'n' have polis alerted at every port atween 'ere 'n' Ireland. Th' jimmy thay call Bear, th' one wha was shot 'n' survived, refuses tae blether. Parntly ya two girls made an impression oan him, as he does keep asking if you're okay. So, at this point, though we knu thare ur aye many loose ends, 'n' we knu thare ur ithers involved, we hawp th' threat tae ye haes bin muchly reduced. That doesn't mean ye shuid be traivelin aroond th' pubs in toun bragging aboot it," he said, then laughed cheerfully and once again raised his glass toward the two girls.

May Ling looked to Sean, Kay, and Elise.

"So then, are you heading back to San Francisco right away? And, Pistachio, I'll assume you're off to Jamaica?"

Sean, with a tight-lipped smile, shook his head.

"No. We now know there is a map that points the way to my family's treasure out there. We don't know where it is, but it does exist. A treasure that may be a chest filled with worthless trinkets, probably mud by now, or a fortune in gold, I don't know. If nothing else, there's a book in all of this. We've agreed amongst ourselves to stay awhile and see if we can figure it out. Honestly, we don't have a lot to go on other than we know there is a letter to prove that there is a map and that a lot of people thought my Seanmhair had it. She didn't, but there must be some more clues floating around out there."

Sean took a second to think, thumb pressing into the flesh of his cheek as he rubbed his chin.

"I wish you had caught that asshole, Shaw, so we could drill him about the letter and get our hands on it. Then we could feed him to the fishes."

May Ling looked at Akio, then back at Sean.

"Not that he wouldn't make good fish bait, but odd that you would suggest what appears to be the same fate as the two Japanese assassins."

Sean, a quick study, answered, "May Ling, that's funny, well not funny, but I was thinking the exact same thing when I said it. Remembering what we were told about those two Japanese assholes who got what they deserved. I lose no sleep over believing they might have been disposed of in the ocean. Don't know for sure, don't care. And it wouldn't bother me in the least to learn Shaw suffered a similar fate."

Akio smiled. "I said it before and say it again, Sayōnara.

Ferguson nodded. "Agreed, Akio agreed."

May Ling squinted her eyes with an *I know you know what happened* look toward Sean.

"If that is what happened to them, I agree. They deserve to be fish food. But I'm a detective at heart, and I won't be satisfied until I know for sure what happened so that I can sleep better. And I would prefer it to be the authorities feeding them to the fish after a trial. Ya know? So, for now, Danny, Akio, Sean, Kay, Elise—" she held up her beer, "—Sayōnara, assholes. I wish I could stay and help. Sounds like the adventure of a lifetime. Not that you haven't already had that. It sounds to me like you have yourselves a real-life Hardy Boys mystery novel going on here," she said with a huge grin.

"Ah, no. You mean Nancy Drew, right?" Elise asked.

"Yeah, I vote for that, Elise. But, like the DCI warned you, be careful. Don't go bringing attention to yourselves. We're not absolutely sure we have them all on the run," May Ling warned.

Trying To Return To Normal

Jack took Isa into town, so she could buy Elise some clothes. Nothing fancy, just jeans, a comfortable cotton shirt, and new underwear, all things she could wear while working around the farm. Anything would be better than the torn and soiled dress she had worn throughout her ordeal.

Home before Elise, Kay, Sean, and Pistachio had finished their chores, they laid the clothes out on the twin bed Elise was sleeping on in the room she shared with Kay.

Isa eager to show Elise the surprise went out to the back porch and called James to bring Elise in. When she came into the house, Jack smugly, with a tilt of his head toward the hallway, suggested she go look in her room.

Elise was beside herself, seeing the new clothes. She let the old dress fall to the ground, tossed her old underwear in the room's little trash can, and put on the new clothes. Feeling more alive than she had in weeks, she then strutted out into the living room, pretending to model the clothes, one hand behind her head and the other on her hip.

She thanked Isa, giving her a hug and a kiss on the cheek, and then gave Jack a hug.

"Thank you. Thank you. I love you all. I'm keeping my old dress. A reminder, you know, of grandma and this entire ordeal—no, make that 'nightmare adventure.' Oh, and as a reminder to be more aware of my surroundings. Duh." She said, smacking her forehead with her hand and laughing.

Jack gave her a longer-than-normal hug. "Wur juist glad ye 'n' yer dress ur still here with us." The look he gave her said much more.

James watched the unusually special attention Jack

155

showered on Elise and quickly deduced what was going on. *They're attracted tae each ither. I'll be damned,* he thought.

A natural jokester, James saw this as the perfect time to go back to his room and gather up some of his old, loose-fitting clothes, jeans, and a t-shirt, to give to Sean, poking fun at his brother and Sean.

"Ere Sean, ah thought mibbie ye cuid use some freish, old clothes yersel', as those skinny-malinky ticht jeans, 'n' ticht fitting rid plaid shirt have ye, weel, lookin' a wee out a place 'ere in th' country." He laughed and handed Sean the clothes.

Kay was laughing so hard she was coughing. "Right," she said.

"What? It's the latest lumberjack look all the techs wear in Silicon Valley," Sean replied, taking the clothes. "But, yeah, I do feel like I kind of stand out more than I should here. So, thanks, even though I know, you're just making fun of me."

"Hon, those perfectly coiffed beards and tight jeans they all wear is sillier than hoodies and saggin'," she said, nudging him with her shoulder. "Oh my God, go put those on. Please," Kay begged.

Clues From Beyond

They spent several days working on the ranch, relaxing with a heavy or two here and there while discussing how they might find the map for which men were willing to kill. On the third day, they were taking a break at lunch, all of them sitting around Isa's big table in the kitchen. Sean set down his beer on the table with a peculiar, quizzical look on his face and was about to ask something when Elise let out a long, heavy sigh.

"I'm so happy both of you were with my grandma when she passed, that she wasn't alone. I wish I could've been there to hold her and say goodbye."

"Elise, you and I are going to visit her grave as soon as we get back to San Fran—" Kay stopped and cocked her head. "Wait a second," she said, and then reached into her pocket and pulled out her cell phone. "Elise, I don't know if you want to or even should see this. But I have a video of when your grandma passed. It was an odd moment. She was talking to Sean, and I didn't think she was going to—No. No, wait, I'm sorry I brought it up. You don't need to see it."

"YES! I want to see her. I don't care if it's tough to watch. I want every second of my grandma I can get." Elise blurted out.

Kay held the phone for a second, debating if she should, but finally agreed. If it were her grandmother, she would want to see it as well. She held up the phone and pushed play.

Elise started crying instantly, seeing her grandmother but chuckled when she saw her grandmother move Sean aside to spit her chew on the floor. Then everyone heard her say to Sean, "Sàbhail mo Elise, cuir am falach an ganzie agus marbh na h-uilebheistean sin."

Wiping tears from her face, Elise told Kay, "I'm so glad you recorded that. Thank you for showing it to me."

Isa looked at Kay. "I'm glad ye teuk th' video as weel, Kay. It does mah hert guid tae see her one lest time. Whit she tellt ye Sean is: *Save mah Elise, hide th' ganzie 'n' murdurr them monsters.* 'N' if ah knu Katharine, she wis telling it lik' it's. She wants they men deid."

Elise, still wipping the tears from her face and sniffing as she did, said, "*Ganzie* just reminded me of something grandma told me. Ganzie means sweater, by the way. When the two of you left our booth at the fair, Grandma looked at me oddly and whispered, *'The lad does not know it, but his ganzie has something hidden in it. Isa would know.'*"

Isa got that light bulb just turne on look on her face. "Go an git yer jumper, yer ganzie, yer sweater, whitevur, all three, Sean," she laughed. "'N' bring it intae th' scullery whaur thare is guid light."

~~~~~~~~~~

"You know, Pistachio, your mom sort of, in a roundabout way, hinted that we might see something more in this sweater than stitches and cables. And you, Isa, you already see something, don't you? You recognized something odd the first time you saw this sweater. Right? Is there a hidden message from 500 years ago in this sweater? Maybe it will tell us where we can find the map everyone is looking for," Sean said as he smoothed out his sweater on the large hand-hewn kitchen table fit to belong in a Viking's longhouse.

Isa made her way around the garment, touching it like she was reading brail.

"Jack, fetch mah magnifying gless wid ye."

Jack returned with an old-looking glass with a bone handle and a lens about five inches in diameter. Isa looked for a good five or six minutes without saying a word, just an occasional, *hmm...*

"Ere. It starts 'ere," she said, pointing to the right sleeve's cuff. "Tis a lang message," she said, finally looking up. "Durin' th' war, ah worked wi' th' British airmie. Ah was originally juist thare tae hulp wi' whitevur thay wantit. Bit whin mah commander found oot ah knitted he sent me tae Belgium tae hulp read th' codes hidden in knitting. Thay actually hud a netwurk o' older wummin wha sat at th' train stations 'n' knit th' schedules o' th' Nazi trains 'n' whit thay wur loaded wi'," she said, not looking up from the sleeve she was studying.

"Och, look thare, wull ye," she said lifting one sleeve to expose the sweater's armpit. "That shuid be that bonehead Kitchener stitch making th' graft a' smooth." She stopped and spat on the kitchen floor before delivering a tidbit of knitting history, "He wis th' British Secretary o' State fur War, back then, 'n' stole th' stitch 'n' gave it his name. Whit a butthead." She let out a "hmpf," then continued. "Bit see, it's nae. See it's a' lumpy nae smooth. Thare is even mair written 'ere." She smiled, knowing this could easily have been missed and that she had found what may well be the most important part of the hidden messages.

"Fetch mi some paper 'n' a pen," Isa told Jack.

He returned and handed her the paper and pen.

"Na, ye sit 'n' write 'K' fur knit 'n' 'P' fur purl as ah say them."

Jack nodded and prepared himself, leaning over the tablet with a pen at the ready.

"Oh my God! It's like some kind of binary code. These people invented binary code when they were still fighting with spears on horseback. That's incredible," Sean said, standing as close as he could but enough out of the way so as not to interfere.

Isa started a rhythm, almost singing. "Knit, knit, purl, purl, purl, knit, purl..." that lasted for just over three hours, taking only short breaks. Every time she stopped, she put a small clip into the knitting, so she wouldn't lose her place. Finally, she looked up, "James, grab us a' a heavy. That's th' lot o' it."

Sean and Pistachio looked at the paper, filled with a seemingly meaningless bunch of Ks and Ps.

"Now what?" asked Pistachio.

Sean was staring, near hypnotized by the long list of Ks and Ps. A computer coder, he was already seeing patterns.

"Hang on," he said and ran to the room Isa was letting him stay in to grab his laptop and ran back excited by what he saw.

"Sorry, Jack, would you read those back to me?" he asked, then added, "Slowly."

Jack complied, and while they all sipped on their beers, Sean typed in the code. It took nearly an hour to repeat it all. Sean then converted the Ks to 1s and the Ps to 0s. He smiled, looking at something more familiar. "See right here, the three 0s in a row. We keep seeing that everywhere. My guess is those are spaces between words." Converting the three 0s to spaces made it look even more binary-like. "Now, correct me if I'm wrong, but this isn't going to be in English. What did they speak? No, more importantly, what language did they write in during the fifteenth century?"

Isa took a large drink of her beer, then told James, "Anither round. Aye we have wirk tae do. Th' maist common leid spoken 'n' written was Gaelic. Ah knu some, bit ah don't think enough. Mi dear mukker, Bonnie, wha speak 'n' writes th' auld leid very weel. Jack, she fancies ye, kin ye gang see if she wull come ower again?"

Jack returned with Bonnie much quicker than any of them expected.

"Whit's a' this aboot codes tae buried treasure in th' knitting o' this jumper?" she asked, walking through the door, giving Isa a hug, then James.

"James, be a laddie 'n' git Bonnie a heavy."

Before James could even say yes, Bonnie asked, "Cuid ah have mibbie a wee bit o' Scotch, if ye have ony handy," being polite but knowing full well they did. It was the MacDuff household, after all. James returned with a glass, the bottle, and a smile, knowing well Bonnie's love of Scotch. He poured her a small glass and handed it to her, watching as she gently touched it to her lips before turning it up and emptying it into her mouth.

"Mibbie a wee bit mair, James?"

~~~~~~~~~~

At first, they looked for what might be determiner or article types of words. Finding two that appeared to be 'tha,' they moved on to looking for numbers, knowing they were trying to decode a message about a map, and again it appeared they found 'try.'

It was early in the morning, and the cocks were crowing but with eighteen possible letters and several more rounds of Scotch, they had a rough enough draft that Bonnie was able to fill in the missing pieces.

"Às an sin bidh na Sìthichean a' bathadh ann an lochan de shiubhal gorm le drùchd na maidne a' ghrian a' lasadh nad aghaidh dà mhìle is dà fhichead tuiteam gu mullach Bruach na Frìthe. Tionndaidh air ais agus air ais thèid thu, ceud trithead 's a trì a' tuiteam air an druim gu stìoball Am Basteir. Is ann leatsa a tha an saoghal gu lèir ri chumail dìreach gu h-ìosal anns a' ghleann purpaidh far a bheil beairteas Òir Mhoireasdain domhainn ann an uamh."

Which she then translated as:

*"From where the Fairies bathe in pools of blue
travel with the morning dew
the sun lighting your face
two Scots mile and forty falls to the top of
          Bruach na Frìthe.
Switch back to and fro you'll go,
a hundred and thity-three falls
along the ridge to the spire of Am Basteir.
All the world is yours to hold
just below in the purple valley
where deep in a cave
lies the wealth of Morrison gold."*

"Oh my God! Oh my God! This doesn't tell us where the

map is; it is the map! We don't have to go look for it. I've been wearing it the whole time," Sean said excitedly, but his excitement was short-lived, remembering how his Seanmhair and Katharine had died for what was hidden in this sweater. And remembering that it was almost responsible for taking Kay's life as well, he muttered. "Does anyone know where the Fairy Pools are?"

Isa, James, Jack, and Bonnie all said, "Aye!" at the same time. James went on to explain that the Fairy Pools are a big tourist spot, a handful of small pools on the Isle of Skye at the base of a mountain range.

"Ah knu right wur that is. Ah was thare lest munth wi' a braw lassie fur a hike."

"Then it's not a fable; it's not a story, it's true. Ella Morrison made a sweater that her husband, Rory, was wearing when he was murdered and thrown into the sea. This sweater. She must have recovered it from his belongings and taken it with her," Sean said, grabbing a handful of the sweater on the table. "And it's the map to the Morrison Clan's treasure. Holy shit, can this really be true?" Sean asked, mouth ajar, eyes wide open as he glanced at everyone in the room.

Pistachio looked at Sean. "Suh let mi git dis straight. Da Scottish sailor who cum to Jamaica an get mi great, great, great, grandmother pregnant he da sam guy Rory? Da one who was married to da Ella n get har pregnant? Di mon, he get roun."

"Yes, Pistachio, the same guy, our shared ancestor." Sean said, nodding.

"Di gyal is the same one who fine him dead on da beach? An den wen to Merika wid da map to staat ah new life wid har son? An da map was da sweater yuh hav bin wearing dis wul time? An nuh one kno? Whoa dude!" Pistachio said, going from heavy Jamaican to contemporary skater English.

Sean, still nodding, "Yes. Yes, we just don't know the timeline of when Rory returned from Jamaica. Obviously, Ella was living in the Aran Islands long enough to learn their style of knitting and enough time for Rory to return and get Ella pregnant before he was killed. I wonder why someone killed him?"

"So then, when do we go look for the treasure?" asked Elise, ecstatic about the prospect of having something to focus on other than her grandmother's murder.

"Yaah wah goin da be a very rich man Sean, eff wi find dat treasure. Rich an famous." Pistachio said, exposing his brilliant smile.

Sean leaned onto the table to look Pistachio directly in the eyes. "Pistachio. You are a Morrison. Be it mud, dust, or gold; if we find anything, it is equally ours."

Pistachio's smile grew so that it brightened the room. "Yaah wah rare man, Sean. A gud man."

"No, Pistachico, he's the best man." Kay threw in, putting her arm around Sean's waist and hugging him.

In Search of Treasure

The happenstance adventurers took their time planning how to start the search, carefully deciding what they would need. They then took additional time to allow Elise and Kay time to heal before taking on the long slog they had planned. James explained it would be more like a backpacking trip, and they would need tents, sleeping bags, food, and water. Not to mention shovels and picks to use when they reached the spot. After the lengthiest discussion, deciding what to do if they found anything—would they take anything? Could they take anything?—they unanimously agreed they would only take one or two artifacts. Those items they would have checked for authenticity and then inquire about ownership. They would leave the rest until that all-important question, "who actually had rightful ownership of the treasure?" could be answered. The Morrison family, current land owners, or the government of Scotland?

James felt they would need a minimum of four days because it was a five-hour drive if all went well, passing over several restricted and private roads. Rather than trying to hide their movements, everything was planned to look like a bunch of college kids out for some fun in the mountains above the Isle of Skye. This would make it easier to explain Kay's bright blue hair and Pistachio's dreadlocks and Jamaican accent.

They finally left exactly two weeks after Kay and Elise's return. Wanting an early start on the trail, they left the quaint lodge near Merkadale, where they had spent their first night, just as the sun was coming up. Their hosts, Colin and Fiona, had spent much of the evening with them before they retired for the night. Jack and James had put on a show of brotherly sarcasm and love that had them all in stitches while Fiona kept them well-fed with snacks. In the morning, Fiona wouldn't let them leave without a quick breakfast of fried panko-breaded eggs and coffee so strong it would wake the dead.

~~~~~~~~~~

Pulling into the Fairy Pools car park, they were pleased to see that no one else had the same idea that day. After packing up and heading out on the trail, they were quick to reach the magical Fairy Pools, as it was only a short distance. Kay, Elise, and Pistachio were mesmerized and required some serious nudging to put their packs back on and continue up the trail. A trail that seemed to get steeper at the corner of every switchback.

It was already very warm by the time they reached the base of Bruach na Frìthe, where their route went from steep to *holy shit* steep until almost reaching the top. They then followed the ridge that at first descended before heading back up toward Am Basteir. Upon reaching the monolithic spire, James, who had become the impromptu leader of the expedition, suggested they take off their packs to rest, drink some water, and eat a few snacks.

From their view, as the sweater's directions promised, it appeared they could see the entire world. And sure enough, just to the northwest was a small valley surrounded by steep rocky mountains. Pistachio was the first to point out that it wasn't purple. James explained that the purple was mostly likely heather, which was simply not in bloom yet. Everything else the sweater had told them was spot on.

Tired but excited, the six put on their packs and headed down the mountain toward the small valley; their pace greatly increased, spurred by knowing they were very close to a day they would never forget. Their eagerness quelled as the path disappeared, making the going much slower. They started bushwhacking. Which Sean pointed out was a good thing for them—it meant fewer people. Reaching the valley, and without needing to be told by James, they dropped their packs and didn't hesitate to start exploring every inch of the small valley, stopping only to eat some lunch and discuss what each had found. Which, in a word, was nothing.

Undaunted, they continued for several more hours before stopping to set up their tents and prepare dinner. The view from where they set up was spectacular. The grassy meadow was filled with wildflowers busting at the bud to expose themselves to spring. A small stream ran through the middle, prompting Jack to suggest that in the morning, they search the water's source because it might provide more cave openings. In the meantime, James headed over to a spot out of sight to relieve himself. Unzipping his cargo shorts, he heard an odd noise close by. Head tilted toward the noise; he listened until he recognized it was a helicopter.

No sooner had he made that distinction than a blue-and-silver chopper rose from the north just above where he was standing. Still not alarmed, he was looking at the occupants when he saw they had guns. Not one to ask questions when guns were involved, James turned, zipping up at the same time, and ran back to the others, yelling for them to run.

Sean and Kay, not understanding, were confused by the

loud noise and surprised to see James yelling and running toward them. They started to walk toward him when they saw the helicopter land just beyond their tents. But now it was too late—there was nowhere to run. With no weapons and nowhere to hide, all they could do was watch the start of a new nightmare unfold.

The pilot stayed in the helicopter as two men jumped out. One holding an AK-47, the other a shiny chrome pistol with a white bone grip. Over the noise of the helicopter's whirring blades, the man with the pistol yelled at them to gather together in front of him.

Sean mumbled, "Oh crap. The Japanese mafia is back."

Kay looked at Sean. "They're Korean."

"None, a yous, needs to get hurt. Just give me the map, and I'll let you leave," the shorter man with the pistol yelled as his hair and clothes were blown about.

Sean watched as the other five all turned their heads toward him, knowing that he did, in fact, now have a map. Sean surmised that the map no longer mattered. They knew where they were and could find their way back. The only thing he could think of doing was to put on a show, so he begrudgingly removed the paper with the directions on it from his pocket before walking forward, instinctively ducking because of the blades. He handed the short, greasy but well-dressed Korean man the paper.

The man smiled, and then, looking toward his accomplice, he waved his pistol toward Kay.

"Stuff the Chinese chick in the helicopter," he said, pointing the pistol at Kay, sounding like he had watched too many gangster movies. Sean started to step forward to protest, only to meet the muzzle of the pistol turned horizontal and pressed against his forehead.

"We're takin' hers with us. When we find the treasure and have it safely in our possession, I may jus' let her go. It's a really ups ta you. Now, all of you need to leave now, ya get my drift," he told them in his extremely odd Chicago-Korean accent. He then became very serious and mean-looking, pointing and poking the gun at them, and said, "If yous call the fuzz, the blue hair dies!"

As he spoke, from his left side, a complete blur of color in the form of Pistachio hit the man with the AK-47, knocking him to the ground and sending his gun tumbling toward Jack. Jack dove for the gun at the same time, James and Sean headed toward Kay and the man with the pistol. As the Korean turned to grab Kay and pull her toward the helicopter, he fired a round toward them. James heard the whiz of the bullet go by his head, followed by the sharp crack of the round going off from the pistol, stopping him momentarily in his tracks to ensure he had not been hit.

With the pilot's help, the short man was able to drag Kay onboard the helicopter. The pilot held her with his arm around her neck and placed a handkerchief over her mouth and nose.

Kay could smell the damp chemical-laced handkerchief and tried to hold her breath.

The pilot returned to his seat, leaving Kay to be held in place by the short man. Sean, seeing his only opportunity, jumped onto the landing strut, reaching for Kay in a valiant attempt to pull her out. The short man turned the pistol toward Sean and fired a round point blank into his chest, sending him flying backward off the strut toward the ground.

Kay, succumbing to the ether, her world fading to dark, could do nothing but watch in horror as Sean, eyes wide open, fell backward toward the ground, blood spraying out of him, as the helicopter rose into the air.

James dropped to his knees next to Sean, then looked up to watch Kay disappear as the helicopter quickly gained altitude. Jack and Pistachio heard the shot but were wrestling with the other Korean. As they pinned him, they saw the helicopter descend over the ridge and out of view.

Elise ran to where Sean was lying on the ground. She gasped loudly, holding her hands to her mouth. Then, like James, she dropped to her knees. She didn't hesitate, ripping off her new shirt, and not for a moment considering she had nothing else on underneath. She folded the shirt up and laid it over the wound, leaning on it to apply pressure.

"I brought a first aid kit. It's in my pack. Get it!" she yelled. James ran, grabbed her pack, and brought it over to rummage through until he found the small black case with UCSF School of Nursing stamped in silver foil letters. *Aye she's a nurse, that's good*, he thought and handed it to her.

"We have to stop the bleeding and not let him slip into shock." She took a moment to look at his wound more carefully. "He's lucky. It was a clean shot that went all the way through under his clavicle. You're going to be okay, Sean," she said, looking into his scared wide-open eyes as she applied another bandage where the bullet exited. Elise knew his fear was not for himself but for Kay.

~~~~~~~~~~

"We need to get him to a hospital now. Call DCI

Ferguson and tell him we need a helicopter up here," Elise told them, stepping into nurse-in-charge mode.

Sean sat up. "No. No, you heard them, *no police*. They will kill her. I can walk out of here. I'll leave my stuff here. It's mostly downhill after we climb back up to Bruach na Frìthe."

Elise displayed the most painful look, knowing he was right and that this could very well be a choice that killed one or both of them.

"Fuuuuuuuuuck!" she yelled. "Okay, but when we get off this mountain, we still need to get you to a hospital, even if a gunshot wound is going to have the police at your bedside asking questions," Elise said, grimacing, knowing she was right.

"You're a nurse, right?" Sean asked. "Just patch me up and get me some antibiotics. I'll be good. No police."

"First, I'm not a nurse. I was studying to be one but quit to take care of my grandmother. Second, I do remember a class where we talked about gunshot wounds versus stab wounds. Gunshot wounds are far better, well, if you survive the initial impact. The bullet is hot; it sanitizes and cauterizes the wound passing through. Stab wounds do just the opposite, dragging all sorts of debris into the wound. So, if we get you back, and you don't pass out, and if by morning, your shoulder isn't the size of your butt, swelling from an infection, then we, I mean Isa and I, can take care of you. But mark my words, it's a bad idea. I'm only in agreement because I don't want anything to happen to that precious woman who saved my life."

Pistachio, now speaking in almost perfect English, reminded them, "Wi hab another problem." He pushed on the subdued Korean's chest, eliciting a yelp. "Wi need tuh turn him over tuh DCI Ferguson. I tink if wi call him an explain the need tuh be ah secret he will be able tuh help. Yes?"

171

"Good. Then he might be able to get Sean in the hospital where he belongs," Elise added.

"Leav everytin. We kin mak' quicker time wi'oot it. 'N', if need be, James 'n' ah kin tak' turns carrying Sean," Jack said, still carrying the AK-47, and headed to his pack to get his headlamp and knife. "Grab whit yi"ll need 'n' let's git goin' it be gettin' mirk soon."

~~~~~~~~~~

Elise's assessment of the bullet cauterizing the wound had not been entirely accurate; Sean passed out several times. Elise did her best to stem the bleeding, changing the bandages several times on the journey back. They reached the car after dark only with the tenacity of Jack, James, and Pistachio, who took turns carrying Sean as they wound their way off the mountain using their headlamps. Everyone was covered in blood and looked like they had just left a gruesome murder scene. As they got into the car, in a lucid moment, Sean smiled and said, "thank you," before passing out again.

"He is going to need to go to the hospital now," Elise firmly told them firmly.

"I'll pat this asshole in th' trunk fur noo," James said, shoving the Korean toward the open trunk. "Mak' a sound 'n' i'll cut aff yer tongue," James told him as he pushed him into the trunk and shut the lid. Then in an afterthought, he took a moment to survey the parking area to make sure no one else was there to see. He was relieved to see it swas till empty.

As Jack drove, James picked up his cell phone and called DCI Ferguson, explaining the day's events, that they needed to get Sean to a hospital, and that there could be no police involved even though they had a prisoner.

"Oan mah wey. I'll be thare in an unmarked polis motor afore ye git thare 'n' prepare evebody. Pairk at th' rear o' th' hospital whaur th' warkers pairk." Ferguson hung up, grabbed his keys, and told the front desk sergeant he was heading home for the evening.

Jack drove like he was participating in the Isle of Mann time trials, actually getting air off several rolling rises in the road. Jack smiled, thinking their prisoner must be enjoying his ride. At the hospital, they did as Ferguson instructed, parking in the rear of the building next to an older model sedan. Ferguson and several nurses were already rolling out a gurney for Sean.

Ferguson said to a barely conscious Sean, "You worry aboot making it thro' th' nicht sae Kay haes someone tae catch up wi` whin we fin' her. 'N' Sean, we wull fin' her."

He turned to the remaining four. "Ye guys look lik' crap. I'll see if th' nurses kin howk up some gowns fur ye 'n' mibbie git yer clothes washed. We don't need ye attracting ony attention." He didn't miss that Elise was wearing Jack's shirt. It was far too big for her, and Jack was bare-chested. "Ye did weel tae git him doon that mountain 'n' 'ere. If he lives, it wull be by yer efforts. Weel dane. Noo ye said something aboot a prisoner."

~~~~~~~~~~

173

DCI Ferguson returned in the morning after spending the night interrogating the Korean prisoner.

"How's ur laddie daein' this mornin'?" he asked, waking all four, who were still wearing blue hospital gowns and were sitting in various uncomfortable positions in the chairs of the hospital's little waiting room.

"He's going to be fine. Lost a lot of blood, but the wound itself isn't life-threatening. They said he might be able to go back to Isa's later today," Elise responded. "What did you learn?"

"I'm very glad tae hear that. Weel. In a cell, faced wi' murder charges, he sung lik' a littel birdie. Seems ye all managed tae stumble on th' muckle laddie his-sel, Hyun-Ki Pung. He is th' Korean crime boss spearheading th' entire bootlegging operation. Born 'n' raised in Chicago, he moved tae Korea in his late twenties, whaur he joined yin o' thair syndicates, fast as fuck becoming th' crime bosses. Seems he is th' one in possession o' th' letter fund behind a painting. This entire escapade leavin' a trail o' murder is a hobby tae him. A hobby th' guy said that became Pung's obsession."

Ferguson continued, "And, our prisoner wis a' tae happy tae give us whaur he believes thay wull have taken Kay. Though truthfully, I'm betting Hyun-Ki Pung, knuing we have his cohort, wull be smart enough tae knu he wid blether. I'm aff tae reinterview Bear, see whit he knus. Kin ah poke mah heid in, or is he sleeping?"

"Sleeping. We'll tell him everything when wakes up. Thank you," Elise replied.

Singing Like a Canary

A motorcycle pulled up in front of the house, and a man and a woman got off. In light of recent events, James stepped out onto the porch holding his favorite varmint deterrent, a twenty-gauge Browning automatic.

"Kin ah hulp ye?" he asked as he watched them take off their helmets.

Ferguson removed his helmet, smiling at him, "Nat wi'th that in yer hauns," he said, pointing his helmet toward the rifle.

"DCI Ferguson, sorry. Wur aye bonny shaken by a' o' this. Daein' oor best tae be careful," James replied, lowering the rifle. By then May Ling had her helmet off. "Weel aren't ye two a pair. Didn't knu yer rode."

"I don't, Jack!" May Ling responded, running her free hand through her short hair. "He just scared the livin' bejesus out of me on that thing."

"Aye, we ur bein' careful as weel as we tend tae staund oot in this toun in oor normal polis ehicles. Ah thought mah scooter 'ere wid be fine disguise," Ferguson said, walking up onto the porch. "How's Sean daein'?"

"It's James, May Ling. Baith o' ye c'moan in. He's in th' living room bein' a real pain in th' bahookie," James said and laughed.

"I'll never be able to tell you two apart. You redheaded Scotts all look the same. Add on to that; you're identical twins..." May Ling chuckled.

She followed James into the house and immediately walked over and gave Sean a hug, being careful not to touch his shoulder. Then she smiled. "We have some news. We believe we know where they're holding Kay."

Sean's face lit up. "Really?"

DCI Ferguson sat in a chair facing Sean.

"Aye, we dae. Mah interview wi' Bear went exceedingly weel. Th' furst thing he asked whin a saw him wis, '*how ur th' two girls?*' Whin ah explained Elise was fins 'n' safe, he wis visibly happy. Bit whin ah tellt him th' Korean, Hyun-Ki Pung, hud kidnapped Kay, he became th' best informant ah have ever worked wi'. He wanted na considerations except tae hulp."

Elise, smiling, said, "There was something about him that was different. He was never rough like the others. I didn't fear him like the others. It's good to hear he is being helpful; I feared I was suffering from Stockholm Syndrome."

"If you think you are, you're too rational to be suffering from it. You're a tough, intelligent lady, Elise. Katharine would be proud of how you've handled yourself," May Ling told her, then continued with what they had learned.

"Ferguson here brought me in and allowed me to talk to Bear. And, yes, he's smitten with the two of you. He has turned out to be a wealth of information. He told us Hyun-Ki Pung has several places in the UK. But the one he would most likely take Kay to is an old castle he converted into a mansion. It's a fortress and has multiple ways to escape, as well as places to lock someone up and hide them. We have an officer working with Bear, now drawing a map of the property and the rooms he knows about."

"We have set up surveillance aroond th' property tae watch every shift he makes," Ferguson added. "Tell thaim aboot Shaw."

Isa came in from the kitchen. "Oh mah. Whin did ye a' git 'ere? Kin ah git a'body something tae dram?"

"Thank you, but no, Isa, not while I'm working," May

Ling responded, then turned back to Sean. "The RAF found Shaw's yacht. It was floating adrift and abandoned just off the coast of the Isle of Skye. The high-speed tender boat, which is more of a drug-running cigarette boat, and normally kept inside the yacht's internal boat garage, was missing."

"Shit, em got away?" Pistachio asked.

"Maybe. See, they did find one of the crew floating in open water on an inflatable pool raft miles away from the boat. He was totally incoherent, going on and on about ten or twenty Kelpies, he called them that, and the Blue Men of Minch, sea monsters that rose up out of the ocean and climbed onboard. The man has obviously lost it, but he claims that the Kelpies and Blue Men kept repeating limericks and asking them to finish the last lines or they would kill them and sink the yacht.

Apparently, the monsters got angry when no one knew the answers to the riddles and started eating them. Yeah, I know, I know. " May Ling shook her head. "Several of the men jumped overboard, and the rest ran down to the runabout and fled. The man we found was quite proud of himself for grabbing the pool raft and abandoning the ship. We have him on special watch back at the station." May Ling turned to DCI Ferguson, "You get that a lot around here?" she asked sarcastically.

"Weel, frum whit I've read, it's not as streenge as San Francisco," Ferguson shot back. He then licked his finger and pretended to move an imaginary overhead billiards' scoring bead to indicate one point for him.

Fighting Demons with Demons

"Hey madda. Yes, she has bin kidnapped again by difrent people dis time. Ah Korean crime boss named Hyun-Ki Pung. Yah. Nuh. Nuh. They think they kno. Dem a goin' do two raids. Da firs one will hit ah nightclub Pung owns. Da idea is tuh distract him while da second raid goes down at his home. He has an old castle converted tuh ah mansion. One o'clock inna mawning. Eff mi git more information mi wi call. Yah da more da betta. Please do. Tank yuh madda," Pistachio finished, hanging up his cell phone.

"Can she help again?" Sean asked hopefully.

"Mi glad yuh have made da transition tuh seein' there is more tuh these Voodoo rituals dan most people todeay undastan," Pistachio responded.

"You know Pistachio; I took theatre for one and only one semester. One line I learned that I always liked. It is what Shakespeare wrote in Hamlet, *'There are more things in heaven and earth, Horatio, than are dreamt of in your philosophy.'* This, Pistachio is a perfect example. What did your mom say?" Sean asked, his anxiety clearly showing in spite of his attempt to be philosophical.

"Shi already knu Kay eena trouble agin. Shi a bringing togedda ah larger group ah Vodouists. Dem a goin' to hold it at the old Catholic Choch. Madda kno the priest well. Shi seh he will even hold an afternoon mass tuh pray for Kay, before shi sets up. The Voodoo and Catholics di be tight in Jamaica."

Sean patted Pistachio's shoulder. "Only in Jamaica. Wow, but thanks. Come on, let's find out if Isa was able to get ahold of Bonnie."

They found Jack and James engaged in a brotherly,

178

sarcastic tit-for-tat over their laptops.

"Don't mean to interrupt your fun, but did Isa ask you to contact Bonnie about tomorrow night?" an anxious Sean asked.

"Aye, she did, 'n' aye she wull," James responded, then pushed Jack away from his laptop, telling him, "I'm right 'n' ye knu it."

"Ah knu you're a horse's bahookie," Jack fired back, laughing as he said it. He turned to Sean.

"Nae only did we blether tae Bonnie, 'n' aye she is comin' ower th'morra afternun'. Bit as we wur talking, she tellt us she hud many maore fowk 'n' several lairge covens that wid participate if thay didn't live so far awa'. Then oot th' blue she asked us if we knew about—what did she ca' it—oh she said, bam, slam or boom. James 'n' ah baith said it at th' identical time, 'ZOOM?'"

James picked up, "So urr ye ready fur this? We ur now set up tae Zoom th' entire night's ceremony. We have contacted 'n' tested a Zoom meetin wi' all o' thaim. Thare wull be some forty-five participants a' ower Scootlund. Th'morra night Pung's ears wull be burnin'."

Sean, who lived on Zoom back home in San Francisco, could only shake his head in disbelief. He was witness to the preeminent app of the day, created so that the technical specialists of Silicon Valley could work from anywhere, and was now being used to hold a ritual using concepts of witchcraft that dated back to the fourth century. *You just can't make this shit up*, he thought to himself.

"I hope more than his ears will be burning."

~~~~~~~~~~

DCI Ferguson appointed two leaders for the raid because it was just too much for him to orchestrate on his own. His long-time friend, Angus Anderson, whom he had known since their youth (they met in the military and spent many years together at Scotland Yard), would lead the same teams that had participated in the earlier raids. Needing more manpower for the first of the simultaneous raids, Ferguson requested help from Glasgow and from the Edinburgh Police Scotland. Their leader's name was Deputy Chief Constable Rory Stewart. May Ling and Akio would serve as communications liaisons between the two groups.

The teams did their best to lay out to scale the incomplete floor plan Bear drew and from earlier drone surveillance. They well understood there would be surprises. Their biggest concern was that they had no idea where Kay might be held hostage. The property was littered with small buildings, both old and new. Bear did his best to remember where the underground tunnels were but admitted he was not sure how many there were or where they all might be. The best in the business, they knew they needed the element of surprise and a whole lot of luck.

A Fortress

Hyun-Ki Pung's architectural addition to a centuries-old stone castle was nothing short of an abomination. Sharp angles of white stucco, crowned by a brilliant red metal roof, clearly indicated his disregard or even disdain for the history and natural beauty of Scotland. But Bear was right; it was a fortress. Around the property was an eight-foot wall with rolled razor wire stretched across the top, an electronically controlled metal gate, that opened up to 100 yards of no cover before reaching they could reach the entrance. Multiple barred windows provided space to watch and repel any unwanted guests. Cameras and lights were at every corner. No one just snuck into this place.

Ferguson, his friend Angus, Rory, May Ling, and Akio watched the high-altitude live drone footage, looking for the best way to attack the fortress. Their hope was that the earlier raid on the nightclub would ruffle Hyun-Ki Pung's feathers enough to cause him to make errors in his decisions, allowing them to execute an operation that would be a complete surprise. This would allow them to subdue Hyun-Ki Pung's men and rescue Kay quickly. The reality, being broadcast back to them from the drone, quickly dashed those hopes.

"This is goin' tae sound extreme fur a polis operation, bit I'm thinking we drap our men in usin` parachutes. Th' guy haes th' wirst eye fur architecture, bit certainly knus how tae build an impenetrable compound. Th' ither option is we set aff charges at th' back o' th' hoose 'n' then uise th' armored assault tank tae bust thro' th' gates 'n' motor straecht in from the front," suggested Angus.

Ferguson thought about it for a moment, then shook his

Knitting in Jamaica   Gary Thomas Edwards

head.

"We have na airborne or paratrooper qualified men. So yer second option may be th' only wey. It's juist they're oot in th' open fur so lang. 'N' comin' in th' front we telegraph oor intentions, given thaim time tae grab Kay 'n' tak' her elsewhere or murdurr her. Ah don't lik' th' wey it unfolds."

Akio, slightly bowing to the three officers planning the raid, offered, "You will pardon my inexperience in such matters. But it occurs to me that the exact opposite might work to our advantage. They surely are expecting us. So, Uhm, what if we were to fire concussion grenades from the front into the house as we drive the armored assault tank through the gate exactly rike they believe we will, while at the same time, special forces quietly go over the wall in the back? We give them what they are expecting and where they are expecting it. They'll panic; send ar their men to the front entrance."

Angus was the first to respond. "Brilliant, bloody brilliant. Ya' waant tae come wirk fur us?"

Rory nodded. "There's yer plan. It's a guid one. It puts boots inside quicker, looking fur oor hostage's location."

"Gie th' word 'n' we'll be running it thro' th' paces th'night," Angus said, looking at Ferguson for a nod.

"We have bin peepin' wi' a drone. Thay haven't made a move on whaur th' treasure is so we knu Kay is maist likely still thare. Th'morra night, let's dae it!" Ferguson said confidently.

Baron Samedi

"It's on for tonite. Two raids. Da firs a start at one-o'clock inna mawning wen da nightclub a jus a start tuh close up. An da second, the raid on Pung's house, starts at fifteen minutes afta one. Da mansion wi think Kay a be held eena is located jus north ah St Phillans near Meigle Bay. Tank yuh madda, mi will," Pistachio finished and turned to Sean. "Dat was pretty scary. Shi seh shi hav spoken with har Voodooists eena Haiti. Dem will be holding their own rituals on da island eena three separate temples. Shi did tell mi dem a goin' da dark Voodoo. Summoning Baron Samedi. Shi seh his name an let out da scariest laugh mi have evah heard. Mi think shi hav already let da spirits tek ova har body. An by spirits, mi don't mean jus rum."

"Who is Baron Salami?" Sean asked, eyes furled in a what-the-fuck look.

"Oh, mon, it's Samedi; he, not a deli meat. You know hem; he would be the skeleton that wears a top hat and tails. He is death."

Sean didn't know whether to laugh or scream. But he held his emotions in check. Tonight, he would cut a deal with Satan himself to save Kay.

~~~~~~~~~

Agwe finished talking to her closest friend in Haiti, who

would convey all of the information to the rest of the Voodooists participating in the evening's combined rituals.

Agwe showed up at the Catholic church that her friend, the priest let her use. Aware that Agwe would be conducting a Voodoo ritual, he never asked any questions and was never around when the rituals were occurring. The Catholic church and Voodooism in Haiti and Jamaica often crossed into each other's world, respecting each other's religion.

Agwe arrived at the church with a car packed full of everything she would need as dusk set in. She wanted to be set up, so she could start promptly at 7:30 pm.

Once she and those helping her had everything set up, Agwe opened a bottle of rum, taking two large swigs. "Ayyyyyyyy," she yelled, shaking her body and head, and passed the bottle on.

Darkness fell on the old church grounds, and Agwe went outside to light the candles on the back patio. In the yard below, her friends had a large fire roaring in the pit that overlooked the ocean. Here, she set up her altar, just past the fire with the ocean as the backdrop. Once again, she was barefoot and wore the all-white clothes she had worn at the last ritual.

At 7:33 p.m., drummers started playing soft syncopated rhythms at first, getting louder and louder. They would play continuously throughout the evening into the morning hours.

A gathering of over twenty people, mostly women, formed a circle around the fire. They all danced to the rhythm of the drums as they passed the bottles of rum around while chanting to three entities: Maman Brigitte, the loa associated with death and, fittingly, a descendant of a Celtic goddess; Baron Samedi, Brigitte's husband; associated with death and resurrection; and Ogun, loa of justice.

As they danced, Agwe threw a cup of alcohol on the fire, soaring the flames into the night sky. As the flames brightened the scene, she recited a Roman Catholic prayer to start the ritual. They continued to dance and chant to the three gods until nearly 8:00 p.m., all while Agwe drew her symbols on the ground with yellow powder.

Agwe disappeared, returning with a rooster in one hand and a machete in the other. She danced around wildly, spinning in circles and screaming her chants in Langaj until she stopped suddenly, and with one quick blow of the machete, she severed the head from the rooster, tossing the head into the fire. Still holding the rooster's squirming body, she screamed "justice, justice, justice" at the top of her lungs to Ogun, whom the sacrifice was for. She finally stood still, her arms raised to the heavens, and let the rooster's blood run down her face.

Zooming The Guardians

Jack and James started earlier in the evening, making sure everything was set up correctly and was ready for the evening's event. They felt like a film crew, setting up lighting and cue marks with duct tape to ensure everyone knew where to stand when it got dark or crazy. They even had Bonnie test the cordless Bluetooth lavalier mic she would be wearing. They practiced several times walking around and videoing the creation of the circle and welcoming of the Guardians until they were comfortable they could successfully share the ritual with those Zooming in to participate.

As the wee hours of 12:30 a.m. drew near, they watched as, one by one, individuals from all over Scotland and Ireland logged on to their one-of-a-kind Zoom meeting. James sat at the keyboard, welcoming each guest. Sean was again in his robe, but this time with his arm in a sling. His shoulder throbbed painfully because he had not let it rest since being released from the hospital. He paced the yard until Pistachio, also in a robe, came over and coaxed him into joining him at the table where he could play the lute and Sean could watch without interfering. It would be better if they stayed out of the way and let those who knew what they were doing help Bonnie and Isa. Tonight there would be considerably more people in Isa's backyard than there was room for. It mattered not, as Bonnie wanted as many participants as possible. She knew there was great power in large numbers where all held one collective cosmic consciousness.

"Bonnie, ye kin stairt whin you're redy, ah have every bodey logged on 'n' peepin'," James told her.

As embers from the fire filled the night sky, Bonnie repeated a ritual that was very close to the one she had done previously, except there were more people both there and across Scotland and Ireland repeating the Eolas she chanted. Earlier in the day, she had taken the time to prepare a new poppet of Hyun-Ki Pung that was passed around while everyone chanted his name. But on this night, when they finished the ritual, she threw the effigy into the fire.

Déjà vu

Kay woke up, her head pounding, and found herself experiencing the most depressing déjà vu for some time before the fog finally lifted in her head, and she could look around her dimly lit prison. Her new home was a dark and dank stone cellar with a dirt floor and failing shelves ready to drop the dusty old wine bottles loosely arranged on them. And, if only to complete the horrific scene, there was an occasional rat scurrying by, curious if she might have any food. She kept eyeing the bottles, considering if she could grab one with her hands tied behind her back.

If I break it, she thought, *I might be able to cut the rope.* Not knowing where she was or even what day it was, hungry and thirsty as hell, she wanted out. There was a door behind her that allowed in the dimmest amount of light. In front of her was a short tunnel with another door that she could see had a padlock on it. Trying to focus, she was suddenly overcome with a vision of Sean falling away from her, blood spraying out of his chest.

"Oh my God, Sean, my baby's dead!" she screamed as loudly as she could, wanting the world to feel her pain.

With the searing heat of revenge burning through her bosom, she became incensed and more determined than ever to get out and find the Korean. "I'll skin you alive—you—you—asshole. I will kill you!" she screamed, even louder.

She sat down on a barrel that leaned against the wall. Upset, horrified, and grief-stricken, she started to cry. It was then she saw a familiar sight. Fog started to flow in through the cracks the light used.

What the honest-to-God fuck? she thought.

Things That Go Bump In The Night

Team Two, with Angus leading, started to position themselves around the mansion as the ocean fog started to roll in. *Odd*, Angus thought. *Fog this time of year. Hmm.*

Inside the house, hell was awakening. The fog started seeping in through the fireplace and cracks in the poor craftsmanship of the windows and doors. Hyun-Ki Pung told his men to find out where the fog was coming in and stop it. But it just kept getting thicker.

"Build a big fire; the heat will make it go away," he pointed to the newest member of the gang, Ji-Hoon. The kid, wearing a bright red shirt with an Anime cartoon character on it, jumped up and headed for the fireplace, lighter in hand when an apparition of fog flew by him. He turned to follow it, stunned to clearly see a dragon that stopped and landed, now standing near the fireplace.

"What the Ssi-Bal is that?" he asked, looking at Hyun-Ki Pung, seriously freaked out by the sudden appearance of the foggy apparition.

Pung, just as stunned, got up from his chair and walked toward it, only to have it dissipate into the fog pervading the house.

It was then that his phone rang, and he learned from his nightclub manager that they were being raided. The manager told him it looked like the entire police force was out there, arresting patrons and emptying the warehouse where all their alcohol was stored.

"Shit, what the hell is going on?" he said as the translucent dragon again appeared, flying around the lofted ceilings in slow motion, flapping its huge wings and swirling the fog into hypnotizing concentric circles that seemed to go right through the walls and ceiling. Again, the foggy apparition settled on the floor, then strutted about like a monstrous raven to finally stand next to the fireplace, its eyes glowing red and its nostrils flaring.

Hyun-Ki Pung, who had come to power by being someone who was never shy about using his firearm, pulled out his pistol and squeezed off a round. The dragon disappeared, leaving only a hole in the wall where the bullet exited into the kitchen, striking the oven's gas supply line and ricocheting off the various appliance, leaving a trail of stainless-steel dents.

Pung laughed. "I think we scared our phantom away. Light that fire, kid." The fog was now thick enough that they could no longer see the other side of the room as four ghostly wolves made their appearance, partially materializing out of the mist. They slowly circled around the room several times as Ji-Hoon and Pung watched, mesmerized. Then, walking between Pung and Ji-Hoon, they walked right through the wall Pung had put a bullet in.

"Come with me," Pung said, grabbing the kid's red shirt and positioning Ji-Hoon in front of him as they walked around the corner and into the kitchen.

Ji-Hoon, more than a little apprehensive walking into the kitchen following the ghostly apparitions, stopped and lifted his head to take a whiff of the air.

"Smell like, ah, dead bodies in here."

Pung, sniffing the air and listening, asked, "What is that hissing noise? Shit, what now, snakes?"

It was then the lights went out, and the room went black as night. Instinctively Ji-Hoon, still holding the lighter, held it up and used his thumb to light it.

~~~~~~~~~~

The raid at the nightclub had been going on for at least fifteen minutes. Back at the mansion, Angus and his men watched from outside. They could barely see through the intensifying fog. But it was clear, inside the house, there was suddenly a great deal of commotion as lights started to go on in different rooms.

Angus looked at his sergeant. "Ah, dae believe they're aware o' our wee surprise in town."

Using his phone, he sent a text asking for a welfare check on all positions. Everyone texted back: *ready*.

Keeping an eye on his watch, Angus, concerned about the fog, gave the signal to cut the power to the building. When the lights went out, he waited for a brief second, then gave the order to fire the flashbang grenades into the house, which was immediately followed by an enormous explosion, lighting up the night sky and knocking Angus and several of his men to the ground.

"Whit th' hell kind o' flashbang grenade was that?" Angus asked as he got up, dusting himself off and turning his head to the side to pop the joints in his neck.

"Ah didn't git if off. Ah mean ah didnae fire any grenades intae th' hoose yet, sur," the shocked officer replied, still holding the rifle loaded with the flashbang grenade.

Fair Folk of Scotland

The explosion was so powerful that it crumbled the small building Kay was in and knocked her out cold. She regained consciousness several minutes later to find herself lying in broken glass, and a small lake of wine, pinned under a wine rack with the roof caved in on top of her. *Well, I did ask for a broken wine bottle*, she chuckled to herself.

With that thought in mind, she reached around behind her until she found a piece of glass. Struggling under the weight of the debris for some time, she was finally able to move her hand back and forth with the glass against the rope that bound her. Exhausted, wanting to give up and cry, she thought to herself, *I got nothing else to do*, and laughed determinedly. The feeling of the bonds suddenly pulling apart was overwhelming, and she burst into tears.

It felt like a replay of what had happened before, lying there in the thick fog and hearing gunshots. Only this time, there were lots of gunshots, which proved to be a great motivator. With her hands-free, she was able to crawl away from the wine rack and roof debris to a spot where she could get on her hands and knees.

Craving something to drink, she tasted the wine puddled on the floor. *Shit, that's not half bad.* She grabbed an unbroken bottle and smacked it on a rock next to her, breaking the neck off. Carefully raising the sharp edge to her lips, she took a sip. Satisfied it was okay, she took several big gulps before tossing it aside to break up amongst its brethren.

I have to get out of here. As the thought passed through her mind, the fog started to swirl upward until it became a Fair Folk, a fairy, or a spirit. Like the wolves, this apparition was composed of fog and completely transparent. The fairy, dressed in a thin-laced sparkling gown that allowed her wings, lit with glitter, to flutter, beckoned, almost as if in slow motion, for Kay to follow.

Kay looked to where the fairy had disappeared and could see that the door, previously padlocked, was now lying on the ground with the rest of the debris. Beyond was blackness, except for the subtle light given off by the fairy. Seeing no other options and hearing only gunfire behind her, she crawled in. Still on her hands and knees, in front of her, she saw the fairy and the four wolves that had slept near her, protecting her in the Highland night. The five apparitions gave off just enough light so that she could see there was room to stand up.

The fairy again silently beckoned for Kay to follow, which she did, walking between the wolves. It was too dark to tell which direction she was going, but she could differentiate between the inclines and descents. It didn't take long for the sound of gunfire to completely fade away as Kay walked deeper into the cave. Suddenly, she felt a rush of cool, fresh air gently blowing on her face.

The fairy led them around a corner, and then they were standing outside looking up at the stars. Kay took in a deep breath of freedom and then looked around.

They were on a cliff, with a path down to the ocean on her left and a shrine of sorts, composed of brightly colored rocks mixed in amongst the stones made to build it, just to her right. The fairy waved to her, the fog trailing off her hand and arm, beckoning Kay toward the shrine.

There, Kay was astonished to see several blankets neatly folded and stacked next to the shrine. Feeling a fragile sense of being safe for the first time since her second abduction, she laid down, pulling the blankets over her. The four wolves, once again, began circling her, keeping an eye out. The fairy walked to the shrine, flittered up into the air, and disappeared into the now-dissipating fog.

Tears began streaming down Kay's face as she thought about Sean being killed while trying to save her. It was too much. Wishing she had grabbed a couple of the bottles of wine to drown the pain, she could only sob until her nightmare finally gave way to sleep.

Burn Pung, Burn

Lying in wait for the house to go dark, Special Forces reacted instantly the moment it did. They were already over the razor wire and dropping in on the other side when the blast went off, knocking several of them from the wall to the ground. As they regrouped, trying to assess what had happened, they saw Pung's men fleeing an inferno and headed directly for them. The Special Ops leader yelled for them to stop and drop their weapons. They chose instead to fight their way out.

Out in the open and visible even through the thick fog, the Koreans panicked, running in different directions, looking for cover. The first one to find cover then opened fire on the Special Forces men lying in the dirt or hiding behind trees.

That first shot instigated a horrific firefight. The gun battle went on for twenty minutes while the building behind burned hotter and hotter, flames reaching into the sky, with explosions continuing one after the other as the fire found new fuel.

From the front of the house, Angus gave the order to take the tank in, with his men following behind. The only resistance from the front of the mansion was the fire itself. It was far too hot to drive through, so they worked their way around the side to help Special Forces.

The Korean gang members were no match for the highly trained and heavily armed Special Forces teams. When more officers showed up on the side of the skirmish, and most of the gang were injured or lying dead, the gunfire stopped. A white flag rose from behind a large concrete planter urn.

The quiet was remarkable. As the silence set in, the fog

lifted. Those who could still walk came out with their hands up.

The gang was quickly rounded up and cuffed, then the team leader called for support to help with the fire. Moments later, a helicopter that had been hovering just off the coast arrived, dropping buckets of water on the fire and then left to get more water.

By morning's light, all that was left of Pung's mansion was ashes. Ironically, although his ultra-modern building was gone, the old stone wall of the castle stood defiantly, as it had before Hyun-Ki Pung came along to defile the history of this beautiful countryside.

Police searched for hours after the fire crews were finished. Poking around in the smoldering ashes, they found no sign of Kay or Hyun-Ki Pung.

Tired and exasperated, Angus finally put in the call to DCI Ferguson, who then informed May Ling, who in turn decided it best to drive over and talk to Sean in person.

"I'm so sorry, Sean. The raid went badly. The mansion was completely destroyed by fire, and they can't find any trace of Kay. They can't say she was ever there, but they didn't find her at the nightclub or warehouse, either. It doesn't look good. I am so, so sorry." May Ling hugged Sean, who stood at the front door silently, in shock.

He took a deep breath, "Please tell me they got that Korean mother fucker, Pung. I can't believe she made it through the first kidnapping only to be kidnapped again and die in a fire. FUUUUUUUUUUCK!"

"Pung was there when the fire broke out, and they've accounted for most of his gang members either killed, or that surrendered, but no Pung and no sign of a younger gang member named Ji-Hoon. It's believed they and a third member perished in the fire. The fire was so hot they doubt they'll ever find any evidence that would yield enough DNA for positive identification. So yes, I think they got him," May Ling said, still holding both his hands. "Sean, we don't know that she perished in the fire. We will keep looking for Kay in hopes they had her locked up somewhere else."

Was it Just a Dream?

A loud snap made Kay sit up and look around, pulling the blanket around her tightly. She saw that the grey wolves that had been sleeping next to her were now on their feet and circling. As they did, their very essence dissolved into the early morning air, creating a low-lying layer of fog. Kay's attention was drawn toward the movement within the fog circle being formed. A man, hunched over, was creeping toward her.

A stubby little man, made even shorter by crouching, he was one of Pung's henchmen who had survived and escaped. When he saw Kay and knew he had just stumbled on his passage to safety. A hostage.

As he approached, the fog thickened. Made uneasy by the sudden fog rolling in, he removed a knife he kept hidden against his calf in a small leather holster. Standing up taller, he rushed Kay and grabbed her, sliding behind her and bringing the knife to her throat.

"You be a quiet and do as I say; you might get out of tis alive. You my ticket out of here, little girl," he said, his breath heavy with alcohol.

Shit, what next? Kay thought in horror, feeling the cold steel blade against her skin. "Okay. Whatever you say. Please don't hurt me. I will help you escape any way I can," she answered, trying to appease him and buy herself time.

The fog had become so thick that Kay could barely see her own hands. Without warning, directly in front of Kay, the fairy that had led her out of the cave appeared, hovering four feet off the damp meadow grass. Kay felt a surge in her soul, a glimmer of hope, but also felt the man behind her tighten up, pulling the blade against her throat.

"What the fuck? Who you?" the astonished man stammered. "Go away, or I cut her throat," he threatened.

There was a burst of light, and the fairy rapidly increased in size until it was the giant dragon, eyes glowing red, that had flown through the house and caused so much mayhem earlier. As it flapped its huge wings, the man panicked and pushed Kay to the ground, running off in the opposite direction into the thick fog. At the last second, before he could stop himself, he saw the edge of the cliff overlooking the ocean as he tumbled off, falling to the rocky beach below. There was a scream that died out, then nothing. The fog and the dragon receded, disappearing.

The sun was rising, painting the tall grass green and yellow where an emotionally and physically drained Kay lay next to the shrine, tightly wrapped in her blankets. The four wolves lay near her, resting but watchful. Drifting off once more, Kay thought *it was a dream. Holy shit. That had to be a dream!*

~~~~~~~~~~

Pistachio called his mother to update her on the evening events gone so awry. Sean, in a state of severe depression, still found it within himself to ask Pistachio to tell his mom thanks for everything she tried to do.

"Ello Madda. Nuh. Nuh. Nuh. Nuh, it did nuh go well at all. Deh did a huge firefight an da building wi thought Kay was held eena blew up. Dem did nuh able tuh fine any signs ah Kay. Wait what? Nuh really? Where? Sean git mi ah pad an something tuh write wid. Hold on, okay?"

Sean brought him a torn piece of paper and a pen he found in the kitchen, where a very somber Isa was still cleaning up from the night's rituals.

"Okay go ahead. Yeh. Yeh. Mi nuh kno but mi sure someone here duh. Oh, tank yuh mada. Yuh an angel," Pistachio said, far too happy under the circumstances.

Sean looked at him, his face all scrunched up, not understanding the gist of the conversation Pistachio just had with his mother.

"What did she say to you?" he asked, his stomach churning with anxiety and acid, not really wanting to hear anything else negative.

Pistachio's wide, toothy grin opened up until he beamed. His eyes filled with excitement. "Shi said shi did hav ah vision as they were winding down the ritual at da Catholic choch. Shi tell mi shi did see Kay. An dat shi is a alive. Shi on ah cliff ova a luk da ocean. Shi described ah cave wid ah tunnel dat led out tuh ah shrine ah sum sort. Shi hav ah vision of a fairy girl wid blond hair an ah see thru white blouse. Shi see her hav four wolves watching ova Kay, who was sleeping in ta' grass. She's alive, Sean!"

Sean found it difficult to get excited. Even with all he had witnessed, the reality in his brain was what May Ling had described, nothing but ashes.

"Okay, that would be great news if it were true," he said, head down, exhausted and resigned, thinking to himself, *we both know it's not.*

Isa walked in, overhearing the conversation. "If Agwe says Kay is alive, that she hud a vision, then ah believe her. I'm callin Ferguson." With that, she went back into the kitchen. They could hear her conversation with DCI Ferguson; it went much like Pistachio's conversation with Sean.

She came back out. "He is a stubborn jimmy. Och hell thay all ur. Bit he is aff tae contact th' SARDA gang tae see if anybody is familiar wi' a shrine next tae a cave ower lookin th' ocean. He said he wull ca' us back."

No sooner had she spoken than her phone rang. She walked into the kitchen and answered it.

"Na ye don't say. Then that wid be guid news, aye? Aye. Ah think that is a grand idea. Tank ya, Danny laddie."

She returned to the living room.

"That wis Danny, DCI Ferguson. He spoke wi' Elora from SARDA, th' lassie wi' th' dog called Dagda wha fun Kay th' first time. He said as soon as he tellt her, she tellt him she knus exactly whaur that place is. 'N' that is very claise tae whaur th' mansion was. He is comin' round tae pick ye, Pistachio 'n' mah wee jimmies up tae go hulp search th' area. So ye might wantae be getting ready," she said, smiling then, like nothing at all had just happened, and walked back in the kitchen.

Sean's eyes showed confusion as a glimmer of hope broke through all the doom and gloom.

"Okay—I guess I'm ready now," Sean said, shrugging his shoulders, not allowing himself to hope.

~~~~~~~~~~~

The five of them made the drive to the coast arriving as the sun was gaining an angle on the day. Elora and Dagda were still about ten minutes away. Getting out of Ferguson's car, they all saw for the first time the completely demolished mansion. No one said a word. They just poked around the ruins until Elora pulled up.

"Hi, sorry that teuk sao lang, ah hud tae finish up th' assignment ah wis workin' oan." Dagda leapt out of the SUV and ran around to meet Elora. His entire body was wagging in anticipation, making it difficult for Elora to put his official vest on. "I'm heading ower tae th' place ah think it's at. Cuid all o' ye follow that path thare up th' coast. I'll catch up wi` ye at th' shrine. I'm aff tae have Dagda fin' 'n' follow Kay's scent."

Still holding Dagda, she held up the same piece of clothing she had used the first time, letting him sniff it. "Find!" she told him, and he was off, nose to the ground. Dagda headed directly over to what was left of the opening to the old wine cellar.

Ferguson didn't so much ask as tell Pistachio to stay with the car in case Kay wandered back. A bit timid about standing amidst so much recent carnage that had taken place just last evening, he watched as the rest did as Elora asked and headed up the path, yelling out, "KAY! KAY.!"

~~~~~~~~~

Kay lay under the blankets in that fantasy world just before the light brings warmth and consciousness. She felt safe and comfortable until reality reminded her in a blinding flash of where she was. Sitting up, she looked around. The fairy and the grey wolves were gone. The sky was a brilliant blue with but a few puffy clouds. She could hear the waves breaking on the shoreline below. Getting up, keeping one of the blankets wrapped around her, she walked down the path to the beach and the sea.

Seeing no sign of the man she had dreamed of jumping off the cliff, she stood and took in deep breaths of the salt air. *Wow, it was all a dream.* The gulls squawking reminded her of home, of days spent at Stinson Beach. But she could not shake the vision of Sean falling away from her, his eyes wide open and the blood. So much blood.

I'm alive! she reminded herself. *I have to get out of here and find the police.* She climbed back to the top of the cliff to look for a path that might lead her to a road. *Surely there has to be a road this close to a beach.* She knew she didn't want to go back the way she came, toward the cave and the horror she heard as she escaped. The memory reminded her just how important it was that she get out of there now.

She continued up a gradual hill through tall grass in the direction of the foothills off in the distance, hoping to find a path or a road. With the exercise of walking and the sun out, it was warm enough that she could take the blanket off. But she wisely decided to roll it up and carry it. She might have a need for it again if night fell and she hadn't found her way back to civilization.

She stopped to take a break, starting to sit on one of several inviting boulders but with a change of heart, decided to push on. It helped quell the horrid visions. Lifting her head and wiping off tears, she heard a dog bark. She hopped up onto the rocks to see if she could see anyone. As she strained to see, using her hand to shade her eyes from the sun, Dagda ran up, sniffed her leg, then sat down and started barking.

"Oh my God, it's you, Dagda." She jumped off the rock and hugged him.

"Weel noo, wull ye looky whit Dagda dug up this time. Guid day, Kay. Urr ye okay?" Elora asked, handing Kay a water bottle. Before Kay would answer, she drank nearly the entire bottle.

"I'll tak' that as a aye, 'where's th' food?' kind of answer." Elora beamed at seeing Kay alive and okay. She pulled her close and hugged her. "You're goin' tae be good lassie, weel if ye kin kindly stoap getting yersel' kidnapped." She was grinning ear to ear as she said it. "Yer jimmy is headed this wey up th' trail. Thay shuid be 'ere shortly. Dagda teuk me thro' th' shortcut ye mist hae used lest nicht. That wis spooky."

Kay looked at her in disbelief. "Sean! Sean is here? He's alive?" Tears rolled down her cheeks as she stared at Elora.

"Oy yea, tha right, ah understand he teuk a bullet tae th' shoulder whin ye wur bein' abducted, bit it wen clean in 'n' oot. He is juist fine."

She gave Dagda a well-deserved treat. "You're such a guid laddie. C'moan Kay, th' path thay shuid be on if thay didn't git themselves lost is right ower 'ere."

They wnet to the path and waited for what seemed like a very long time. "Damn those boys are slow," Elora scolded with a chuckle. "Hauld yer horses. Thare. Thare they are. See thaim juist ower yonder?" she said, pointing, but Kay was already running down the path toward them. *Yup, this is aff tae be good*, Elora thought, savoring the moment for a second time.

Try, Try Again

May Ling returned to San Francisco, and Akio to Japan to take full advantage of the recent events. Hyun-Ki Pung's mansion was a total loss, and with it, a great deal of valuable information. However, his nightclub and warehouse yielded enough information, along with what they already knew from their individual investigations and what was found on Logan Shaw's abandoned yacht, to formulate a plan, a plan that escalated into one of the largest cooperatives of international police in twenty years.

The Scottish, Japanese, Korean, and San Francisco police all participated in a well-choreographed series of raids, targeting both bootlegging and counterfeiting operations that had been under the control of the now-deceased Hyun-Ki Pung. The raids took nearly forty-eight hours to execute, with the first operations in Korea at midnight and ending up a day and a half later in San Francisco. Final toll: millions of dollars in cold hard cash were confiscated; thirty-five businesses, all involved in distilling bootleg Scotch, printing counterfeit labels, and managing the shipping operations, were closed down and locked up; as well as seventy-four arrests from press operators to many of the larger kingpins running the show, were made. Early estimates figured that the raids ended a nearly billion-dollar loss of revenue for the major Scotch distillers.

It would take months to sort out all of the materials confiscated and years to run the arrested gang member through the justice system. DCI Ferguson knew all too well that many, with their money and slick lawyers, would slither away into the night. But for now, they were out of business.

Talking to reporters, DCI Ferguson, in thanking the

international teams that were responsible for the successful raids, mentioned that what he felt was one of the biggest assets to their success came from the crime families themselves. Upon hearing of Hyun-Ki Pung's demise, the infighting between the Korean and Japanese families trying to seize control blinded them to the bigger threat that the police were closing in.

~~~~~~~~~~

Isa pulled out all the stops, setting up extra tables and chairs in the backyard. She and the twins invited everyone who had become family during the roller coaster ordeal. Elora and Dagda, DCI Ferguson, and Bonnie were all there; the only ones missing were May Ling, Akio, and Agwe. Not wanting to leave them out, James and Jack set up yet another Zoom meeting so that they could attend the gathering as well.

It was a relaxed evening, with the smells of barbecued salmon and mutton lofting through the air and lots of beer and Scotch loosening up everyone's ability to embellish the many stories being told. DCI Ferguson finished explaining, for what seemed like the hundredth time, how the bootleggers and counterfeiters were shut down and out of business. And, that those responsible for the murders and kidnapping were either dead or in jail awaiting trial.

Kay and Elise were inseparable, hanging on to each other like a couple of giddy high school girls. They could almost relax, no longer feeling the need to look over their shoulders.

206

It was finally Bonnie who brought up the question, "Whin urr ye goin' back tae look fer yer buried treasure?"

Ferguson spoke before Sean could answer. "I'm confident ye kin continue yer search noo wi'oot needing tae fear bein' interfered wi' any langer. However, 'n' ah say this fur yer benefit 'n' then ah wull say na mair, th' quaistion o' whom any treasures fund belongs tae is goin' tae come up. 'N', a'm ferr certain, it wull be the Scottish government that steps in 'n' claims tae be th' rightful owners. Wanting tae add it tae thair museums o' coorse. So be careful who ye blether tae."

"Blether?" Sean asked.

Jack laughed, then said carefully, "Who you talk to."

"Wow listen tae ye git a' American lik'," James said, slapping his brother on the back.

May Ling's voice could be heard over the laptop sitting on the table. "Maybe you won't find all the treasure. If you get my drift."

"Couldn't have put it better, May Ling," Ferguson replied, bending down to look into the dot of a camera on the laptop.

"I'm sorry, Ferguson, put what?" May Ling responded dryly.

"Right, didn't hear a thing. Sorry, bit slow, whit wi' th' Scotch 'n' a'," Ferguson answered coyly.

"Ah, not talking about this to anyone and only selective treasure finds. Yeah, got it. Good ideas. I'll want to talk it over with Kay because, in my book, it's half her fortune as well," Sean responded to both May Ling and Danny.

Elise looked at Kay. "Did he just, in a very roundabout way, say he wants to marry you?"

Kay laughed, then stopped and cocked her head. "Sean, baby, did you mean you want to marry me?"

Sean walked over and knelt down before Kay looked up into her eyes. "You already know we're spending our lives together, forever. But here, now, is the best possible circumstances to ask you Kaylee Wu will you marry me?"

Kay lit up. "Yes! Yes, of course, I will. And yes, Sean, I already knew we would be together forever. I love you." She then looked over at Ferguson, "You're damn straight that treasure belongs to us, Morrisons," she said, pointing her thumb at herself, then burst out laughing.

Elora sat rubbing Dagda's head as she sobbed tears of joy. This was why she did what she did.

Pistachio held up his beer. "Congratulations tuh both aof yuh. Buh nah tuh rain on anyone's parade, wi looked everyweh up there an didn't fine any treasure. Buh yuh can git sum souvenirs to tek home wid yuh at the airport," he said, eliciting laughter from all.

"Mibbie ye shuid let me tak' anither look at yer sweater. Mibbie ah missed something," Isa said, looking at Bonnie, who nodded.

~~~~~~~~~~

Isa, Bonnie, Kay, and Elise, all together imbibing a bottle of Isa's best Scotch, spent several hours in the kitchen turning the sweater over and around, poking it, and looking at it through a magnifying glass. They were just about to give up when Elise noticed a slight variation between the cuff ribbing and the body of the sleeve. They were not the same.

"That's it, ye'v fun it, Elise," Isa told her.

Isa then once again started rattling off "Ks" and "Ps" as

Kay wrote them down. She took the new series to Sean, who converted it to binary code and then once more went through the process of translating it into words. It was much easier this time, because they already had a key from the first round.

Finished it read: *"Far am feum thu a dhol thairis air aon bhealaich eile agus ceud tuiteam eile,"* which Bonnie translated to, *"Whaur ye mist go ower one mair pass 'n' anither hundred falls.*

" The question was, where did that fit into the original translation? Or might they be missing even more?

After too much Scotch, they decided it best to revisit it in the morning. Jack took Bonnie home, and the rest retired early after Isa heated up leftovers from the prior night's festivities.

In the morning, Pistachio was up early and talking to Agwe on his phone. It was the middle of the night in Jamaica, but she had to call. She told him she'd had another vision, a dream in which she saw a group of men and women dressed in ancient Scottish clothing. They looked like, she said a cross between vagabonds and warriors. They were on horseback and stopped near a large rock spire at the top of the mountains. The man in the lead pointed toward to the left and turned to Agwe in the dream and told her to *go northeast, over one more mountain. The cave is behind the whale rock where the morning's rays first land.*

Pistachio joined the group sitting at the table, all hunched over their coffees, and told them what Agwe had said.

"There, then it goes right here," Kay said, pointing to what they had written down from the original translation. Excited, she rewrote the passage, underlining the new words, and then passed it to Sean. "Like this."

It now read...

"From where the Fairies bathe in pools of blue
travel with the morning dew,
the sun lighting your face,
two Scots mile and forty falls
to the top of Bruach na Frìthe.
Switch back to and fro you'll go,
a hundred and thirty-three falls
along the ridge to the spire of Am Basteir.
All the world is yours to hold
just below
whaur ye mist go
ower one mair pass 'n' anither hundred falls
in the purple valley where deep in a cave
lies the wealth of Morrison Gold,"

"Ye knu, ah member that second mountain. It did have a lower plook, a pass. 'N' 'twas tae th' northeast o' whaur we were," James offered up. "I saw it afore we dropped doon intae th' valley we thought wis th' right one 'n' searched. It's beyond that."

"It would appear we need to go through our equipment; the police were gracious enough to pick it up and return to us. See what we need to replace and repack. Who's up for another adventure?" Sean asked skeptically, not knowing if anyone would be willing to risk their lives again.

All hands were in the air.

"You people are gluttons for punishment," Sean said, shaking his head, but realizing at the same time that this group was his family. "Okay, let's do this. But this time what do you say we bring a metal detector?"

Mum's the Word

They stopped again at the little lodge outside of Merkadale. Sean reminded everyone that "mum's the word," even though they liked the old couple. "Keep to the story."

The couple, Colin and Fiona, were so happy to see them that they made them sit on the porch to talk and catch up. Fiona brought out snacks and dark red Scottish lemonade and then went on and on about all the excitement they had missed when they were there last time. She told them about a helicopter landing out front on the road and then later how cop cars drove up and down the road.

"Most excitement we'd seen in years," she said.

Sean took a drink of the red tea mixture, nodded, and agreed. "Wow, that must have been something. Did you ever find out what it was all about?"

"Th' paper said something aboot a kidnapping 'n' a shooting. Jings, crivens, help ma boab, ye wid think we wur in th' muckle toon," Fiona answered.

Sean chuckled. "I'm sorry, Jings crivens? Muckle toon? I have no idea what that means."

Jack and James had to set their drinks down; they were laughing so hard. "Sean—" James had to stop to wipe his eyes and nose. "I'm sure ye git th' furst pairt, th' seicont was: 'My goodness, you would think we were in the big city.' Or wurds tae that effect."

"Pistachio, the more Scottish I hear, the more your English keeps sounding better and better," Kay said, and they all laughed. "Well, sorry to hear we missed all the fun. But we need to get to bed so we can get an early start. Thank you, both of you. We love you two," Kay told them, blowing them a kiss.

211

~~~~~~~~~~

Fiona got up considerably earlier to prepare a quick breakfast for her new favorite guests. She made it clear she wouldn't let them leave until she had fed them her warm scotch eggs filled with soft-boiled eggs and minced meat, battered in bread crumbs and her own special spices. Served with tea, they stayed far longer than they planned, chatting. Finally, it was Kay who pushed away from the table and apologized as they needed to get going. They hugged and thanked Fiona and Colin, promising to return, then headed off to the Fairy Pools parking area.

"Well, this brings back some painful memories," Sean joked, looking at Kay and feeling so grateful they were here together, enjoying a second chance at searching for the treasure but, more than that, a second chance to be alive.

Elise pulled a small hunting knife from her pack. "This time, I'm going to be more prepared," she said, adding the sheath to her belt.

Jack, hearing her, started grinning as he removed from his pack a 9mm Glock automatic pistol and held it up in the air. "Ay lassie, me too," he said as he stuck the pistol in his cargo pants pocket.

"Well damn, with those and Pistachio's karate, we'll be a force to contend with," Kay said, impressed.

"That's great. Really. But please, please be careful with those. We've had enough brushes with death and dismemberment since we've come to know one another," Sean reminded everyone. "Besides, there won't be anyone chasing us this time."

"Oh, crap, did you really just say that? Way to invite trouble," Kay chided him. "What the heck are we standing around here for? We even know the way this time."

It was much warmer than the first time they had climbed the mountain, but, knowing the way, they were much quicker. At the top, they could clearly see the edge of an additional meadow that lay just beyond the meadow they had searched the first time.

Not one of them wanted to stop and rest. They all felt an underlying urgency to move along. However, they did stop at the top of the next pass, where they could look down at a meadow filled with heather starting to bloom, giving the small valley floor a soft purple hue. To the northeast, as Agwe said she heard the man on the horse in her vision tell her, the mountain clearly resembled a whale.

Reenergized, the six of them started down. It was not to be as easy as they hoped. There was no trail, and the way down was rugged and covered with thick brush. Reaching the bottom, the meadow's edge, they shed their packs and, rather than resting, ran over to where the whale had appeared from above. Sadly, at this level, they could no longer see the shape of the whale.

They did their best looking around. James even brought out and set up the metal detector but couldn't find anything. Exhausted, they agreed it would be best to set up camp, eat some dinner, and get a good night's sleep. Sean, Kay, and Elise all set their phones' alarms to ensure they would be up just before the first light.

Kay wasn't able to sleep at all. Every noise, no matter how slight, jolted her straight up in her bag; sure, more men were coming to hurt her. Sean, on the other hand, was so deep in REM that a bomb could have gone off outside their tent, and he would have slept through it.

Morning came, and the sound of three different ringtones going off at exactly the same time had everyone up, dressed, and outside waiting for the sun. James already had his stove out and water boiling to make coffee as the darkness gave way to a lighter sky in the east. As the first rays started to poke through the rocky crags at the top of the mountain, he walked around, filling everyone's cup with steaming hot coffee. "Sorry, ye have tae dram it black, ah have na cream."

"Tanks, James buh yah now ih not matta as lang as eh hot," Pistachio told him, warming his hands on the mug more than drinking it.

"Island boy can't take the cold," Sean teased.

The lot of them sat watching the spreading light, mesmerized, like Druids at Stonehenge waiting for the first ray to appear.

When it did, they all got up and walked over to the spot, looking around but without seeing anything. It looked like everywhere else along the edge of the meadow.
"Hmmm. I knew this was not going to be easy. Professional treasure hunters spend months and years looking for rumored buried treasure," Sean said and sighed.

Suddenly, there was a shrill beeping noise that sent Kay running to Sean's side. It was Jack with the metal detector, holding it near the spot the sun's rays first hit.

"Holy pumpin' jobby. It's 'ere!!" he exclaimed.

"Grab your gloves and shovels and dig in," Sean told them, then paused. "Don't go crazy. One, we don't want to destroy anything, and two, we need to be able to cover it up when we're done like no one was ever here. Right now, we're just looking for an opening to a cave."

214

Nodding, they all ran back to their packs for gloves and tools. They dug in the general area for about half an hour when Elise screamed, "I've got it! There is one really big hole here, gang," she said from her knees, holding her spade in the air.
They carefully removed the rocks one by one, creating a pile they could remove later.

It didn't take long before the hole was big enough for one of them to crawl in. Kay looked at the twins.
"There aren't any curses in Scottish lore like the Egyptians, are there?" she asked.

James looked at her thoughtfully. "Depends on wha ye ask," he said, then stuck his head and arm into the opening with his iPhone's flashlight on. He withdrew his head and looked at them all, his eyes open so wide the whites were visible all the way around.
"Yer nae goin' tae believe this. Sean, go in 'n' look. Thare is room tae staun up in thare."

Sean turned on the light of his phone and crawled in. "Oh my God," he yelled back toward the opening, where five heads were all trying to peer in.

They all watched a light moving about to the rhythm of grunting noises and shuffling things about. Sean was only inside the cave for six or seven minutes. However, it seemed an eternity before he came crawling out, holding a gold plate under his arm, an ornate gold mug with an antler handle, and a well-worn, modest-looking gold crown; a simple engraved gold band adorned with rubies. The look on his face was a man in shock, and it showed.

"Oh my God. Oh my God," he kept repeating as he handed the plate, the mug, and the crown to be passed around. "It's truly unbelievable how much gold is in there. Gold, swords, body armor, and chests. And it looks like they just laid everything in here yesterday. There were even some wool blankets folded up on the chests. There truly is a fortune here in terms of money and history. My ancestors, the Morrison clan, did well for themselves. Well, at least until they went and got themselves killed by the British."

One by one, they took turns crawling in to survey the bounty. Once everyone had their chance, Sean waved to them all to sit down.

"I've modified our original plan. If this is okay with you, Pistachio. We'll take turns going back in. Each of us will carry out four pieces. Your choice, but keep in mind that you need to carry them down the mountain. Can't be running about town sporting a gold-handled long sword," Sean said, smiling. Seriously though, we then rebury the opening, so it looks like no one has ever been here. If we make it out of here, back to the car unseen. Everyone keeps three of the pieces they find for themselves, and then third, we all combine to hand over to the National Museum of Scotland, explaining our finds. If they're agreeable and willing to work with us, we tell them where to find the treasure. They should know best who holds the rights to the treasure."

"Personally, I would be honored to have it sitting in the national museum, protected and taken care of. Well, as long as we get to keep a couple of trinkets like these for our own family collections," he said, giving Kay a hug. "But first, I want to be clear. Every one of you needs to be onboard." He said and looked at Pistachio. "Pistachio?"

Pistachio, overcome with emotion, could only nod.

"Laddie, th' botuum line is, it's yer family's fortune, yer history. Ah knu ah speak fur Jack 'n' ah, we ur alang juist tae be apairt o' this adventure," James responded.

"Oh, so you're speaking fur me nuw urr ye? Haw, it's

amazing ye kin pat two wurds th'gither, let alone a sentence," Jack said, laughing as he mock punched his brother in the ribs.

Without hesitation, everyone agreed. Then they took turns; Sean first, Pistachio, Kay, and Elise followed by James and Jack. The haul was an astounding array of items from the fifteenth century. Sean went in one more time and came out with a small leather chest. Grinning, he said, "This is too good, and you've all gone through hell and back to get here. Each of you takes a piece of jewelry," he said, and then opened the chest toward Elise, who was closest to him. She gasped. "Go ahead, Elise, take a piece in memory of your grandmother."

Elise, crying, took a small gold bracelet. Each of the others, without saying a word, solemnly took a piece of jewelry. Sean took out a ring with a bold crest on it and slid it onto his finger.

"Hmm, it fits. Must have been one of my great, great, great, great, however many greats it takes to go back that far, grandfathers." He held it up proudly. "Okay, let's pack this stuff away and close up this hole."

The New Normal

"Nuh. Madda seh mi need tuh fly home now." Pistachio explained, arms in the air like the wings of an airplane.

"Surely it can wait a couple more days." Sean protested, wanting Pistachio to stay.

"Nuh mon. Madda seh shi a fraid dis last ritual leff open ah portal ah sum sort, dat is allowing Baron Samedi unfettered access tuh our wurl. Di Haitian Voodooists tell har dem experiencing fur too many gruesome incidents dat can only bi traced bac tuh Samedi. Mi cud hear di fear eena har voice mon. Madda hav nebba shown fear a roun mi as lang as mi hav bin alive." Pistachio said, his voice somewhere between scared, apprehensive, and trepidatious.

"Then Sean and I are coming with you." Kay told him.

Both Jack and Elise were nodding.

"We're coming too." Jack added.

James, shaking his head, put his hand on his brother's shoulder. "Na brother. Yi"ll need tae stay 'ere. Ye 'n' Elise need tae stay 'n' hulp Isa wi' th' chores. Ah wull go wi' thaim."

"Mi duh luv di offers. Buh nuh. Yuh need tuh stay until mi fine out wah is goin on. If mi need yuh help, mi will call yuh. See, dis wah mi luv all of yuh. Madda was very emphatic dat mi cum home now. An, wen madda wants something, mi ave learned it bess nah tuh argue." Pistachio grinned exposing his huge, perfect white teeth.

Sean held up his hand pretending to be blinded by the brightness.

"Dude, warn me so I can put my sunglasses on before you smile."

"Ha. Mi suh glad mi able tuh stay lang enuff tuh help

218

yuh fine yuh ancestor's treasure. Your Seanmhair, shi wud bi prouda yuh." Pistachio said loading his single carry on into the trunk of the car. They had all decided it best if they sent the bigger, more valuable items they discovered, home using an international shipping company to avoid having to explain the unusual items at customs.

"No, Pistachio. What I said before, I meant. You and me, we're family. All of that treasure and any fortune that comes from it is ours. We share, got it?" Sean stated firmly, putting his arms around Pistachio to give him a hug. "Kay and I will come see you and your mother in Jamaica as soon as we get our lives back in order. And you. You my friend, have a room and a bed in San Francisco anytime you want, for as long as you want."

Kay joined in with the hug wrapping her arms around both of them.

"The next time we see you, I'll be a Morrison as well. Let's see, what does that make us anyway? Never mind, that's too hard to figure out, let's just call it what we are, family." She grinned and hugged him again. "I know we got off to a weird start. And never in a million years would I have believed I would be standing here now with so much respect and love for you. I love you Pistachio. You take care of yourself, and Agwe. And, if you need help with whatever is going on, you call." She said, and wiped a tear from her eye.

"Mi luv both yuh suh much. Yuh have giv mi ah huge gift. Yuh hab giv mi bac faith eena people. Yuh hab returned mi ability tuh differentiate between di gud ones an di bad ones." Pistachio gave them both another hug.

"Elise, wow, wah an adventure. Let's nuh du it again." Pistachio laughed, shaking his head, and then hugged her. "You an Jack, need tuh cum visit mi eena Jamaica. Mi will show yuh mi favorite beach." he said with a big grin, turning his head toward Kay

"Just make sure that is all you show them." Kay shot back, laughing with him.

Pistachio then walked over to Isa and hugged her for a long time.

"Tank yuh Isa. Tank yuh fah treating mi as ah member tuh fambily. Yuh a such ah gud cook. Wen yuh cum tuh Jamaica yuh an Agwe can knit, an shi can show yuh Jamaican cuisine." He turned to to James. "Cum an gimmi hug. Wi a brothers yes? An mi expec yuh, Jack, an Elise tuh cum visit mi on mi island. Yuh nuh need as many clothes, buh di three ah yuh bess bring lots ah sunblock."

He got in the car and waved at them, hanging out the window all the way down the driveway as he and Jack headed to the airport.

~~~~~~~~~

James was loading Kay and Sean's baggage into the trunk of the car as the two said their goodbyes. Kay hugged Isa for several minutes. "I will never forget you, Isa."

"Forgoat me. Ah think nae young lassie. Yi"ll need tae return soon 'n' finish yer knitting lessons. Thare is so muckle mair a'm waantin' tae shaw ye. Besides, ye don't waant Elise 'ere getting a wey lot better than ye," Isa said, grinning, and hugged Kay back some more.

Kay turned to Elise. "Are you sure you don't want to

come home first, visit your grandmother's final resting place? Not to mention getting your affairs in order before you disappear over here forever. Besides, we made a deal back there in the barn, remember? We're opening a knitting store in Marin. I had a dream last night about what we're going to call it: *Knitting in Scotland!*"

"Ya know, just a thought, honey, but how about *Knitting in Jamaica?*" Sean threw out.

"Oh my God, yes. It's common knowledge, the tie-in between Scotland and knitting. But Jamaica. That'll stop 'em in their tracks. Brilliant, Sean," said Elise excitedly.

"I agree, babe. You can handle all of our marketing, website, and social media," Kay said and kissed him.

"That's the best idea of all as I need help turning on my computer," Elise laughed. "And no, I haven't forgotten. Kay, you're so much more to me than a knitter I want to go into business with; you're my sister. I love you and will always want to spend as much time as I can with you. And, yes, I'll come back in a few months to visit Grandma, and we can look around for property then. But Isa can teach me so much. And well—" she smiled like a little school girl and grabbed Jack's hand, "—since we now know, thank you, James, for looking it up, that our families are far enough removed that we can—" she giggled, "—well, you know."

"What she's tryin' to say," spoke up James from the car, "Is that thare in looooove," he said, sarcastically drawing out the 'o' and hugging himself and rocking back and forth as he did.

"Fur once, brother, ah absolutely gree wi' ye." Jack turned to Elise. "In case ye didn't knu it lassie, a love ye."

Elise just melted on the spot. Her cheeks glowed as red as a Scotsman's hair as she wiggled herself closer to Jack, wrapping her arms around his waist.

"I think your grandmother would be quite okay with this arrangement," Kay told them. "We'll be in touch, and we'll return soon, Isa."

Sean shook Jack's hand. "Be good to her. Ah, I know you will." Then he, too, gave Isa a huge hug. "Love you, Isa. You, Bonnie, and Agwe made believers out of me. I am forever indebted to you. I just wish Pistachio hadn't left before us. This hug fest doesn't feel complete without him. Ah well, I'm sure he's already back on the beach in Jamaica up to his old tricks."

Kay snorted a laugh.

"A'm needin' tae come tae San Francisco, juist sae ah kin git me some o' they metrosexual lumberjack claes lik' ye wur sportin' whin ye git 'ere," James poked at Sean.

"Oh, yeah, you'll fit right in. We'll get you one of those haircuts where they trim the sides and give you a bun," Sean replied, and they all laughed except Isa, who had no idea what they were talking about.

"Aye, but now, we need tae git goin'. Yer plane leaves in two hours 'n' customs 'ere is a boot," James told them as he shut the trunk.

~~~~~~~~~~

The Airbus A380 touched down at San Francisco International with a jolt followed by a couple more before the jet's reverse thrusters roared, slowing the plane. Inside the terminal, Kay and Sean, relieved beyond words to be home, headed to the parking area to retrieve their car.

"Well, this is going to be expensive," Kay said as they approached their car, which was covered in a layer of coastal dust.

"No problem. I'm sure we're both unemployed after being gone so long," Sean said, smiling before blowing off the dust on the driver's side window and unlocking the car. He then reached down to unlatch the trunk. Walking around, he stuffed their luggage into the small trunk, shut it, and walked to Kay's side, where he stopped to grab Kay's shoulders.

"You know what, Kay? We're alive, we're home, and we have each other," he said, and then kissed her passionately.

Arriving home, they ignored the mess they'd left. They did pull down the crime scene tape that was still fluttering in the breeze. Sean opened two beers and, handing Kay one, asked, "A heavy, my love?"

She smiled and kissed him. "Don't mind if I do."

Sean picked up his cell phone, knowing from the ringtone, the theme from *Colombo*, that May Ling was calling. His heart couldn't help but race as he touched the green button. All of his encounters answering the phone, knowing it was May Ling, had been of the less than warm and fuzzy nature. "Hello. You, too. It's wonderful to hear your voice. Yes. Yes, she is. And you, how are you? Awesome. Not to be rude, May Ling, but if you're calling, it can't be to sell me tickets to the Policeman's Ball. Ah, huh? Yeah. Well, that is good news. More, really? No way. Whoa. I will, and you, too. We need to get together sometime, you, Soomee, Kay and me. I'll buy the beers. Okay, 'bye."

Sean looked over at Kay, who had already started knitting. She set her WIP down on her lap, preparing to listen and watch Sean's face as he repeated what May Ling said.

"Whaaaaaaat?" Kay asked, afraid, like Sean, of why May Ling might have called.

"No. It's okay. We don't have to buy any tickets," he said and laughed. "You're not going to believe this."

"What?"

"Well, first, she said, they've closed the case for the two missing Japanese gangsters in Jamaica. Well, not closed it, but she said it was moved to the missing person file." He stopped to look at her with a grave face. "Babe, I could hear it in her voice. She knows that we know what happened to them. She's just looking the other way because of who they were and what they did."

"I had the same feeling when their names came up at Isa's house. She gave me that *I know what you did look*. It freaked me out," Kay said, nervously fiddling with her needles. "Is that all?"

"Well, I believe she's on our side on this one. As far as we're concerned, there's no reason ever to bring their names up again." He smiled at her and got up to walk over and kiss her.

"That was all?" she asked again.

"No. She also said she had just received a call from DCI Ferguson. He told her they found Logan Shaw." He paused to watch her face recognize the name.

Her face contorted before he finished saying, *Logan*.

"They got him? His sorry ass is in jail? Yay!" she responded.

"Well, no. They found his body washed up on a beach on the Isle of Skye. She said he had been severely beaten, and then he drowned."

"Am I bad for wanting to celebrate?" Kay asked.

"No, babe. That piece of pond-sucking scum got exactly what he deserved, and it didn't cost the taxpayers a dime.

Chalk that one up to the Kelpies, the Blue Men of Minch!"

~~~~~~~~~~

Two months later, James emailed to say Elise missed Kay and wanted her back to learn more knitting with her from Isa. And, that they all missed Sean and Kay wanting them to return for more adventures.

They also brought them up to date; that there was still no sign of the missing Korean kingpin.

Pistachio had called them every week to tell keep them in the loop of the missing Japanese men. That he had heard nothing, a good thing. He told them that the considerable concern over Baron Samedi and an opening to his world turned out to be of no consequence. Life had returned to sun, sand, tourists and pannists playing their steelpan drums in the distance of both Jamaica and Haiti.

During his last call, he told them that both he and Agwe missed them. But, that the important news was that since his return to Jamaica, he had opened his own private detective agency. He now was working out of the back of Agwe's Choch ah Knitting shop, and he had already solved his first case of theft and had been paid for it.

"Shit, it's just going to be another ploy to pick up unsuspecting tourists, especially women," Kay laughed. "Once a Rasta Beach gigolo—" she said, laughing more. "But I love the man. We owe him our lives," she said fondly.

"I agree. Do we need to get him to visit us here, or do we

need to go back to Jamaica? Ya know, check up on him. Kidding, this time we go for fun. I'll even bring the sunscreen." Sean said, trying to imitate Pistachio's substantially wide grin.

"And for knitting lessons from Agwe, of course," Kay said, working on a sweater for herself. A sweater that contained her own version of an embedded code, revealing where she and Sean had buried a cache of two large plastic food buckets with snap-on lids, taped and sealed with paraffin, deep in the Desolation Wilderness of the Sierra. They contained the pieces of treasure they hadn't turned over to the authorities. Something they decided, as their ancestors had, could be passed down to their children's children's children.

~~~~~~~~~~
~~~~~~~~~~
~~~~~~~~~~

If you've enjoyed **Knitting In Jamaica**, *you'll enjoy Knitting's band of protagonists facing a new set of murders at Burning Man. The quintessential setting for all of them to explore and expose to the world sides of themselves they never believed they would. Look for* **Knitting Man** *soon on Amazon or in your favorite Bookstore.*

Made in the USA
Columbia, SC
30 September 2023

23561240R00124